RIDING FOR LOVE

CONTENTS

DISCLAIMER:

Thank you for taking your time to read Riding for Love. As always, I am always looking to expand my artistry. With that, I wanted to try a different genre: Urban Romance. It is not your typical Urban Romance seeing as though, I did my own variation of it. I'm not sure if I'll do a second but writing Grym and Willow's story was refreshing. Although it has a lot of elements that are not part of what I normally write, it still has touches of the feel-good romance that I pride my brand on. Thank you in advance and hope you enjoy

CHAPTER ONE

Grym Jones (pronounced Grim)

"Y ou done yet? I'm not trying to be late."

"I would be if you'd just take a puff." My best friend grunted as he took a pull of his blunt.

"Nah, I'm good."

Green removed the blunt from his smoked stained lips. "Nigga, you act like weed is worse than the D'ussé you be drinking?"

"D'ussé ain't putting me behind bars. Alcohol isn't illegal. That blunt you got in between your crusty ass lips will have me locked up in a cage if we get caught riding around with it. A nigga like me is meant to roam freely." I took the last swig before placing the empty glass on the end table.

"Killing niggas will have you in there for life but that doesn't stop you from doing that, does it? Grym I've seen you take niggas' lives without as much as batting an eye yet you over here acting like smoking a little weed is the worst a nigga could do," Green preached.

His words fell on deaf ears as a smile tugged at the right side of my lips. "Yet here I am G, a free man."

The way I saw it, none of the points he was attempting to make were valid. Yeah, I was an assassin, but I took the necessary precautions to avoid prison at all costs. The only gun that I rode around with—outside of being on an assignment—was my legally registered .45. I wasn't afraid of prison.

After the life I had lived, nothing scared me. But nobody wanted to be controlled or treated less than human. You could ask any nigga in prison and they'd tell you that they rather be out in the free world. I was careful to not jeopardize my freedom.

Green silently shook his head before putting out his blunt. We were in his space, so I couldn't restrict him from smoking. "Let's get this shit out the way. I swear I have to find a new connect because the way this nigga moves, I'm not with it."

I had a strict no drug policy. I didn't use them. I didn't sell them. When he first entered the game, I was right as his side since life had bonded us. Green made his money as the biggest king pin in Miami, FL Typically, I stayed away from his business dealings, only attending meetings at his request. But if Green was requesting Grym, it could only mean one thing.

Green grabbed his keys off the table, and we headed to a secluded location in North Miami. In the midst of acres of dry land and darkness, sat an old abandoned building where Green pulled his truck to a stop. "This is the spot. When we get in here, I'll do the talking. All they need to know is that you're my body guard. That's it."

I nodded my head as I exited the passenger side of Green's black on black Escalade truck. We were in Green's territory which meant following his lead. It was nothing for me to fall back; to assess a situation. Recklessness had never been one of my flaws. Thirty-two years on the Earth and I lived with only one regret.

As we approached the metal double doors guarded by two barely armed men, with my head on a swivel I scanned the area for all possible exits. "We're here to see Santino," Green announced to the men. Their weak ass rifles amused me.

"And who are you?" the shorter of the two spat in a heavy accent. Niggas that were shorter than 5'8 always had the loudest bark and softest bite.

"Green. Get Santino, I only talk to bosses." There was no masking the imminent threat in his tone.

That was what set Green apart from the rest. There wasn't a reason to fear anybody that bled just like him, so there was no person or thing that could intimidate him. We moved the same and that solidified our bond as brothers rather than best friends. We understood the importance of living life fearlessly. And above all; respect. We had both grown up without parents for as long as I could remember we were all we had. To survive the shit life threw at us, we had to live life without fear. Whether it was the fear of death.

And just like a bitch taking orders, he hopped on the handheld radio to inform Santino of Green's visit. What I respected the most about Green was the way he handled his business. When he was giving me the rundown there wasn't anything about Santino that he left out. I was the reason for their meeting, even if Santino didn't know that yet.

Santino cleared us to come in, and the guards let us in without a search. They could've, they looked like they wanted to, but it wasn't going to stop Green or I, from walking in there with our straps. The shorter guard led us to the middle of the warehouse where—who I assumed to be—Santino was standing, between two men. They stood there smug and condescending in their aura, not realizing they had already been caught slipping. I could and absolutely would, take all three of their lives without losing a wink of sleep.

"Green, who is it that you have with you?" Santino quizzed. His Spanish accent was heavy on his tongue. He wore dark sunglasses, but I felt his eyes burning into me.

Allowing Green to take the lead, I listened attentively. "My bodyguard. You sent word you wanted contact with Grym. I have a line to him, that's all we have to talk about."

He smiled sadistically at Green. Anyone could see Green didn't have any respect for Santino, his blatant disrespect was overlooked because their business was too beneficial. "Yes, I require his services."

"What you want?" Green asked, his expression tight enough to warn Santino he wasn't for wasting time.

He turned his head and leaned close to the man on his right. After whispering something quickly and waiting for confirmation, he turned back to face us. "I want a meeting with him."

"Look don't waste my time with the bullshit Santino, you know that's not how this goes. But I'll humor you and explain again. You tell me what it is you want and why. I run him the details, if he accepts, your request will be taken care of."

Santino looked uneasy as his face flushed with redness. Green wasn't going to compromise. I had one rule for this shit. He was the only one who knew what I did in my spare time. Well, there was one other. If and when a body was found, there would be no way to pin me to it. Green was always my alibi, using my cell phone and credit cards in all my favorite spots when I was out on a mission. I made it a habit to keep all my receipts. My tracks were always covered because we were more cautious than most. We knew like everything else, the lifestyle we were living was not the forever plan.

He and I started off in the streets together at sixteen, after meeting in a group home. Where he preferred to sling dope, I loved the rush of my trigger finger pressing onto cold steel. Taking a life came easy to me. The world didn't show me life, so I sowed death back into it. I caught my first body at seventeen when a corner boy tried to stab Green. With each life I collected, I traded piece of my soul. For a while, I'd caught a light and let it guide me. But as quickly as it came, when it was gone, I was left in total darkness.

Life fed us to the streets, and we did whatever it took to survive.

"Very well then. I need him to take care of someone for me. My nephew should not be rotting in a prison cell right now because of his lawyer's incompetence. He promised me he would get him cleared of those rape charges, took my money, and didn't deliver. Now he has to pay with his life."

"Understood. You'll be hearing from me." Green responded and turned to walk out. I turned and followed suit without a second glance to Santino or his men. I could feel them staring at our backs, but I had all the information I needed.

I was strict the way I moved, staying undetected. This nigga was in my presence and didn't have a clue. That was the way I liked it. I was able to decide what assignments I would take. Studying changes of tone, facial expressions, and body language, I was able to pinpoint any signs of deceit. Based on Santino's response, he was very well aware that his nephew committed the rape. He was hoping his money could buy the boy's way out of facing the consequences.

Once we were back in the car I looked over to Green, as he pulled out into the dirt road that would take us back into the city. "He did that shit, and Santino knows it."

"Hell yeah, that nigga did that shit."

As much willing pussy as there was out here, I never understood what would motivate a nigga to pursue an unwilling one. That shit never made any sense to me, and it never would. We were in Miami, pussy came in a variety of shapes, sizes, and ethnicities.

There was easy pussy and put in work pussy.

There was forty dollars pussy, and there was forty thousand dollars in the form of a car, pussy.

There was local pussy, and vacation pussy.

There was no damn reason to go after an unwilling pussy.

None.

"What you thinking? The only reason the old ass nigga

wants his nephew out of prison is because he's his successor," Green stated, as I gazed out the window.

"That nigga has to die. Whether he won the case or not, he signed his death warrant the moment he agreed to defend a rapist."

Wallace Lambert, Esq. was a dead man walking and would soon have the pleasure of meeting the Grym Reaper.

CHAPTER TWO

Grym

Pouring a glass full of Hennessy, I finalized my plans with Green. The kill was going to be simple. I was going to be in the empty building across from his downtown condo. When I had the shot, I was going to take it and forget any of it ever happened. Santino was traveling to the Dominican Republic to avoid being questioned when Wallace's body was discovered.

Green was going to be at dinner with his flavor of the week to evade any suspicion. Although there was absolutely no way that he could be tied into a murder that I committed, we always took the extra precaution. There was no such thing as being too careful.

"Everything is set for the night." I sat in Green's leather recliner in his all black living room hoping to soothe the unfamiliar uneasiness feeling that was creeping up. Never had anxiety overwhelmed me before a kill yet I couldn't completely shake it.

Green took a puff his blunt. "For real Grym, how do you sleep at night? I've killed a few niggas and that's some shit that I can't ever get over."

"With two eyes closed and the temperature on seventy-one nigga."

To say that murdering someone came naturally wasn't true. My first kill was out of necessity. It did however make every other kill that followed, easier to bare. The innocent were never my target. If the streets and the judicial system failed to do their jobs, I had no problem doing so. There were many times that I witnessed grimy niggas get away with shit.

Disloyalty equaled death to me. A person without loyalty was a person that wasn't worry to breath the same air as me. I wasn't a righteous type of nigga. How could I be? I had taken over two hundred lives. To be honest I was numb to death. When you walked around fearlessly, couldn't shit scare you. Killing for hire was just a code of conduct that the pain of life had taught me that I adhered to.

"You crazy as hell bro." Green took another buff and shook his head at me.

"You killing niggas daily, G. You're fucking up families. You have parents abandoning their children every day. How do you sleep at night?"

G had a way of acting like his shit didn't stink. As if he didn't negatively impact our people by poisoning them with the dope he sold. Even if he wasn't on the block slinging it anymore, he was still in the game. The only difference between the two of us was that he didn't have to look into the eyes of his victims. That part was the easiest for me. I lived with my choices I made without them weighing me down. When my victims took their last breath, I made my peace right then and there. Green saw things different.

"Two eyes closed, and my dick in some pussy."

I chuckled at his stupid ass response. Green and I were aware of the consequences of our actions. That was why we agreed on retirement at thirty-five. We made good money and had enough investments to hang it up. We weren't young dumb niggas that went and bought a dealership cash with no resume and no real job history. I had bachelor's degree in finance. Yeah, I was from the hood but I was an educated hood nigga. I wanted more out of life that what we had taken. The only way we could do that was by one day going fully legit.

Years ago, we had gone to the bank for two loans to invest in a few commercial real estate properties, and two tech companies. When the businesses started turning profits, we repaid them with the same loan money we borrowed. The interest was a small price to pay considering how we were really moving. With that fool-proof plan, we kept the pigs off our backs. We had paper trails on top of paper trails for our legitimate businesses.

"You ignorant as hell Green."

"And you need to get some pussy or smoke some weed to relax your ass. That Henny ain't doing the trick."

Ignoring him, I took a gulp of my drink. "Nigga shut your ass up."

That was where Green, and I held differing views. He enjoyed juggling multiple women at one time because he hadn't found the one to tie him down. I on the other hand didn't give a fuck about love, therefore I damn sure wasn't in search of anything from women. A wet dick with nothing to accompany it wasn't appealing to a nigga like me anymore. I valued myself way too much to be involved in that bullshit.

More importantly, I had too much respect for women. It had been over a year since I had been in some pussy. The thought of it alone had me spacing out. If it wasn't the pussy that belonged to that woman, then my hand would get the job done.

"Listen, one day I'm going to settle down, but today ain't that day."

"Tomorrow won't be that day either. What time is your dinner?" I questioned Green.

"Seven. What time you need to be in place?"

"He gets home at six so I'm going to get out of here and set up, within the next hour."

It was going to be an easy kill. I had been watching Wallace for two weeks in preparation. His life was boring and routine. However, the only time he was ever at alone was when he was at home. The condo he lived in took pride in providing top notch security. They weren't anything that I couldn't get through, but required more work than I was willing to put in. I didn't want to take the chances of possibly missing something. I chose sniper mode from across the street, killing him with a long-range shot instead of a long drawn out task. It was going to be clean and easy.

Green and I spent the next hour bullshitting until it was time for me to go. When it came to my assignments, I never drove my personal vehicles. I had an unmarked van with paper tags that I kept in my garage. The last thing I needed was a cop running my tag. Karma was always right around the corner, and I was going to make it hard for her to catch up to me.

When I made it home, I quickly went into my gun room to pick two of my favorite toys. I wasn't sure which one I wanted to use yet. I grabbed a box of bullets from the shelf was adjacent to the wall of guns. I placed them all in my duffle bag and threw it over my shoulder. When I got in the car, I retrieved my laptop from the passenger seat to disable the security and camera systems within a two-block radius of Wallace's. The timer was set for forty-five minutes, giving me enough time to get in, set up, take my shot, and get out as quickly and quietly as I came in.

As soon as I made it downtown, I parked my van a few cars down from the front of the empty building. Taking the stairs, I made it to the seventh floor which would put me directly across from Wallace's condo. Him having all glass windows and no blinds, shades, or curtains was like he was asking for me to come kill him. When I made it inside of the apartment I had chosen, I rapidly set up my tripod and snipper rifle, got into position, and began to wait patiently for my target.

Seconds passed and he emerged from the back and into the living room. As I got ready for the kill, the same uneasiness I felt earlier in the day made its way through my body.

Finger on the trigger, I observed Wallace stalk over to his front door.

I followed that nigga every day for two weeks, and the day I had chosen to kill him was the day he had a fucking visitor? My blood boiled, knowing that I'd either have to wait out his visitor or come back another day. Either way, I had only had about twenty minutes or so to decide.

Wallace opened the front door, granting his visitor access to enter. When he swung his body making more space, I saw her.

My heart shook in my chest.

My hands began to sweat.

My head spun the more mesmerized I became with her.

She was beautiful. Long curly hair grazed the middle of her back. The sun peering through the glass window illuminated her chocolate skin. Her petite frame was visible in the distressed jeans and black tank top she wore. She appeared disheveled, as the two engaged in a conversation.

There was no way that I could take out Wallace with her there. Frustrated, I packed up everything with the knowledge that I had ten minutes before the camera and security systems came back online. Looking back before leaving, two things were certain.

She gifted Wallace another day of life.

She was mine.

CHAPTER THREE

Willow

As my stepfather stood in front of me rambling, I blacked out.

My day had begun normal as any other. I worked as a software engineer. At lunch time, I ate with my cousin Trinity, as I did every day. My regular-degular everyday life never consisted of me sharing space with my stepfather, listening to him rant about the criminals he chose to defend.

"Willow did you hear what I said?"

I snapped out of my thoughts, "No. What did you say?"

"Its best that you get out of town. I can get you a new identity. All we have to do is fake your death."

"Fake my death?" My voice heightened at the crazy plan that Wallace had concocted.

"Willow, sweetie, listen to me. Mistakes were made during the last case. This is the only way I can protect you." Wallace pleaded.

"Protect me? Protect me from what?"

Wallace married my mother when I was eleven years old. They were married for twelve years before she passed away from cervical cancer. At twenty-three years old, losing my mother was the hardest thing I'd ever had to overcome. Five years later, I was still battling, and I lost daily. Time didn't heal all wounds. Acceptance did, and I had yet to accept that my mother was gone.

"Sweetie listen to me, none of those details are important," Wallace declared before walking away, into the kitchen.

After my mother passed he sold the house they'd purchased, to get a condo downtown. I was livid with him at first. He had tearfully explained that he couldn't bare living in the empty house they picked together; only filled with their shared memories. Wallace wasn't a bad stepfather to me growing up. From what I was able to see, he did love my mom.

He and I didn't have a father and daughter relationship, but he was the only father I knew. Therefore, I did have respect and love for him. He did the best he could, being a white man raising a black girl. Of course most of his efforts were motivated by my mother nevertheless, I did appreciate them.

"Wallace you are asking me to leave my entire life behind, fake my death, and change my identity. What the hell do you mean the details aren't important?" I seethed.

If he wanted me to comply, he was going to have to divulge every single detail. He made his career choices; I'd be damned if I had to change my life around because he screwed one of his clients over.

Wallace slammed the refrigerator door shut. His pasty skin was drenched with beads of sweat. "Watch how you talk to me, Willow."

Walking over to him, I threw my purse on the kitchen island. "Then tell me why the hell you want me to leave. Who is after me?"

I refused to back down. If he demanded as much as was he was out of me, he was going to have to answer all of my questions. For as long as I could remember, Wallace was always involved in some type of shady dealings with criminals. It never impacted my life before. If it was going to now, seventeen years later, I needed to know why.

"No one is after you Willow. I'm afraid that someone will be after me very soon. I don't have any proof, but I know how they operate. If they're unable to get to me, I'm afraid that they may get to you. I couldn't live with myself if that were to happen sweetie. I promised your mother I'd take of you."

Disregarding his last statement, I tried my best to empathize with him. "Am I in any real danger as of yet?"

"No but…"

"I get that you're afraid Wallace, and because of that I'll consider it. Take care of yourself, I have to go." Retrieving my purse from the marble top island, I left his condo as fast as I could.

My nerves were beginning to get the best of me. I pulled out my phone to call my only friend, my cousin.

"Hey cousin, you good?" her soft voice flowed from the speakers of my car.

"Trinity, where are you? I need a drink."

"That's a no. I will be at the house an hour."

"Thank you. That works since I'm in Miami."

After agreeing to meet at my house, I ended the call. As I rested my head on the steering wheel, my conversation with Wallace replayed in my head. Maybe I should've been more scared than I was. Instead, I was more annoyed with Wallace than anything. My emotions got the best of me as I thought of how my mother had always been my protector. With only the sound of her voice she would've been able to calm me down, to help me process everything that was happening. When I was finally able to gather myself, I pulled out into the street and drove around for about thirty minutes or so, in case anyone was tailing me.

For Wallace to be an esteemed lawyer, he had horrible decision-making skills. If someone were after him for whatever reason, him inviting me to his condo to discuss it was dumb as hell. I was smart enough to know to get out of there and not go straight home.

The minute I was positive no one was trailing me; I drove to my house in Fort Lauderdale. Trinity's car was in the driveway when I arrived. She and I shared a four-bedroom home since I had moved from Miami. There was nothing left for me there. I couldn't leave South Florida all together, so I ended up less than thirty miles from my hometown.

Trinity was opening the front door with a glass of red wine in her right hand before I even made it to the door. She and I in a favored in appearance, we shared the same beautiful dark skin, and brown eyes. She, however had long locs that hung to her back, and was a few inches taller than me. Trinity was my mom's older brother's only child. When my mom first married Wallace, I spent most of my free time at his house. She was the only friend I had growing up. Although we were different, we protected each other because we were the only family we had left in the world.

Wallace had moved my mom and I out to the suburbs away from Little Haiti. It was the hood, but it was my hood. A part of me still was there and Trinity helped me remember that connection.

"You are wearing the stress on your face," Trinity stated as I took the wine glass from her.

I kicked my tennis shoes off at the door as I entered the house. I tossed my purse onto the couch as soon as I sank into the love seat. Trinity sat on the other side waiting for me to unload what was bothering me.

"Wallace..." Trinity instantly rolled her eyes at the sound of his name. I continued, "Wallace wants me to fake my death."

There could've been a better way to tell her but that was how it came out. Trinity's loud laughter brought confusion. "I swear you play all day, Willow."

I popped out of my seat with my drink still in my hand. "I am not playing."

Pacing the living room floor, I went into detail, recounting the encounter between my stepfather and me. She completely finished her glass of wine by the time my story was done. "Shit, that's a lot."

"Exactly. And on top of that he won't give me any information other than someone may come after him, and possibly me."

"Look, I never liked his rat-faced ass but maybe you should take heed to what he's saying," Trinity reasoned with me.

Snickering I replied, "I can't take you serious when you're calling him rat-faced."

Trinity shrugged her shoulders. "That nigga does have a rat face. All I'm saying is, it's okay to take precaution from here on out. Maybe you should stay out of Miami for a while."

I stopped pacing long enough to pour me another glass of wine. "Trinity you and I both know I don't go to Miami often. The only reason I even went was because Wallace called me panicking."

When I received the call from Wallace, I was doing ninety on I-95. His frantic state had me in my own state of panic. He really never called, which heightened my anxiety while driving down to Miami. "Do you think I should fake my death?"

"Girl hell no. I don't trust that. I say you look deeper into what he was into before you decide what to."

Trinity was right. Wallace was asking a lot from me without giving me any real reason to go along with his elaborate plan. "You have a point. I'm definitely going to look more into it."

Going into my bedroom, I went to get my laptop. Back in the living room, I began my research. I needed to find out what the hell Wallace had going on. There was no way I was going to fake my death. I'd leave, but no one he could be associated with was that powerful.

Either way, I was going to get to the bottom of whatever was going on. There was no way I could permit his mistakes to turn my life upside down, not when I had just gotten it up right side up.

CHAPTER FOUR

Grym

Two days passed since I was supposed to close out the contract on Wallace. I hated having to call Green to tell him that I needed a new plan. Apparently Santino was upset, but I didn't give a fuck about that. If he wanted to go with someone else he could, but I knew he wouldn't. There was a reason he sought me out. Grym was the best of the best and he always delivered. Wallace was the first mishap I'd come across in sixteen years.

"Tell me again how the fuck you missed."

It took everything in me not to knock that nigga's head off his shoulders. I had been ignoring his calls and texts for the past two days. I had to get my mind right. He finally showed up at my house. I appreciated the brotherhood we shared but him sitting across from me currently wasn't one of those times. G helped me through a lot of shit but what I was going through wasn't something that I could share with anyone.

"Nigga I didn't miss shit."

Green threw his hands up, "Okay you didn't miss, but Wallace is still breathing."

"Thank you for the information Captain Obvious. Nigga I know that nigga is still breathing because I left him breathing. I just need to rethink my plan before I go forth with it."

Never in all the years that I spent taking lives did I ever question what I was doing. It wasn't like I didn't know killing was wrong, I simply didn't give a fuck. The fact that they had family and loved ones didn't mean anything to me. Yet seeing her, for the first time I was forced to change my plan.

I was back to following Wallace's every move to ensure that she wouldn't show up again, though a part of me was wishing she would. Even if it was for a minute, seeing her beauty would satisfy a hunger that had consumed me. My mind was focused on ensuring that Wallace's routine wouldn't change but my heart, that muthafucka was praying that she would show up.

"Grym I don't give a fuck what Santino got to say. My issue is with you not acting like yourself. For two days you've been off the grid my nigga. So tell me what's going on."

I sighed heavily as I sunk deeper into my sofa. Rubbing my hand over my waves, I tried to string words together to makes sense of what was going through my head. Normally I could discuss anything with him.

"I was ready to take the shot. Everything was going smoothly. No traffic. No issues with shutting off the systems. Everything was perfect until…"

"Until what?"

I chuckled at his impatience. "Until she showed up."

"Who the fuck is she?"

There weren't any series of words that I could thread together to make sense of who she was. "I don't even know what to say man. I saw her, and I froze. I couldn't take him out with her there, couldn't taint her like that."

That was partially the truth. Yeah, I didn't want an innocent person to witness a death. However, deep down inside, I knew that wasn't the only reason. There was more to it than that. Way more than I was willing to admit to Green, and definitely more than I was ready to admit to myself.

"I'm following him again, to make sure there's no more surprises. I'll take care of it," I assured him.

"I was just fucking with you. You got it, I ain't worried about that. What had me popping up on you was you going missing on a nigga. That's not like you at all."

"Yeah I just had to get my mind right bro."

"Is your mind right now?" Green had a wide smirk plastered on his face.

"Yeah," I lied. My mind was far from it.

"Good. Now we're about to go to this cookout at Marco's, eat some good food, and you can handle the rest of that shit tomorrow."

I needed the distraction, so I headed to my bedroom, threw on a pair of jeans and a black V-neck shirt. After I was dressed, we hopped in our rides, set on unwinding at the cookout. Marco worked under Green and was as loyal as they came. Neither of us grew up in a tight knit family, so we kept close to the one we chose.

When the hustling bug bit Green, I hit the block with him. No matter how many hours he put in, rain, sleet, or snow, I hugged the block with him. The one night I was running late, Green was set up. He was always capable of handling his own business, but three against one were never fair odds, and they got the best of him. G dished out his own damage and was wearing one nigga out to the point that as I approached, another of them pulled his piece, pressing it into the back of G's head.

The expression on my nigga's face as kept his head held high, ready to eat his bullet like a real one was forever burned into my memory. I pulled out at my .38 with no hesitation, releasing the trigger twice; catching both of those niggas slipping and splattering their thoughts on the sidewalk. The only reason the other nigga was allowed to live, was to tell the story of who sent him. When we'd pulled all the information Green's boss needed, he too, swallowed a bullet from my .38.

That night solidified the brotherhood between G and me. We decided that any team we started, would only be treated as family since we never had any. We supported any and everything the team did, from backyard cookouts to business launches. There was strength in numbers and loyalty was always rewarded with loyalty.

A short drive later we were pulling up at Marco's house. It wasn't any special occasion; niggas just found any reason to grill. As long as the weather permitted, niggas was throwing cookouts every day.

The smoke from the grilled filled the air. Uncle Luke was blaring through the speakers. It was a whole Miami vibe.

"What's good G? Grym I ain't seen you in forever nigga,

wassup?" Marco and I shook up.

The team we built knew Grym, the man, and Grym, the assassin. Though, I wouldn't confirm, a few of them hinted at me still being active. My name held weight in the streets, but I was a lowkey type of nigga. My privacy was imperative to my peace. The only time I was around anyone other than Green, was at a random pop up to an event. Those niggas didn't bring me in any money thus there was no reason to be around them any more than I wanted to be

"Been handling business. Laying low."

"Not shit," Green responded.

"That's the only way to do it man. Meat should be done in a minute. Y'all can go ahead and grab a plate." Marco said.

Doing as he said, I observed my surrounding. Most of the people were people we knew from around the way. Some of the guys had brought the women they were dating or at least fucking off with at the moment. That shit got under my skin. I hated the idea of having temporary people around me. It was even worse when the women would bring a friend that was hopeful to find a man with fat pockets. That was some shit I couldn't stand on. I didn't like people enough to be around a bunch of muthafukas I didn't recognize.

"Fuck," G said under his breath.

My eyes followed the direction he was gawking at. There was a tall woman with wide hips and a long weave, walking towards us accompanied by another woman with similar features. "Green can we talk for a minute?"

"Not now Tasha. We can talk later, after I eat." Green

turned his back to her. He began uncovering the aluminum trays.

"Me and my girl Nikki, can fix y'all plates."

"Nah, I'm fixing my own plate," I rebutted. I didn't know either one of those women. Nikki was staring at me, almost like she was fucking me right here at the food table, a clear sign that she wanted to do more than fix my plate.

"Your friend is rude as hell," Nikki voiced.

"What's rude is you invading my personal space. Didn't nobody invite y'all to come stand this close to me," I responded. Usually, I kept quiet, but I had a bad feeling about those two. Green dipping his dick in anything walking wasn't about to fuck up my day. I already had a lot going on.

In true Green fashioned he began to laugh with his back still turned to Nikki and Tasha. "Tasha, I'm going to get back at you in a few okay?"

"Okay," she replied. When she realized that Green wasn't going to say anything else, she walked away with Nikki trailing behind her.

"See, that's the type of shit that happens when you let women that you have no intentions of being with, have hope."

"Man didn't nobody give that girl any type of hope. She was the one I went on a date with the other night. I didn't even fuck off with her."

"Whatever you say nigga."

That was a situation I never wanted to see myself in. I didn't want to walk around giving women false hope. I sure as hell didn't want to deal with the craziness that came with a woman that wasn't getting her way. After witnessing first-hand what Green was dealing with, I knew that wasn't the life for me.

I coveted companionship.

I wanted to create a real family.

I craved a wife and children.

I needed love.

So I elected to do something I would never do; I was going to go after her.

CHAPTER FIVE

Willow

As I sat at Press and Grind Cafe during my lunch break, an unknown number popped up on my screen. It was the same number that had been calling for a couple of days. It would call a total of two times a day. Never left a voicemail or a text message. With everything going on with Wallace, I was on edge.

The first time the number popped up on my screen, I answered but the other line was silent. After that, I ignored the other three calls. Wallace hadn't made any effort to reach out to me since I visited his condo. I wasn't even upset because it was best that I kept my distance. Wallace's confession was becoming stressful. I was choosing different routes to and from work.

"Hey cousin." Trinity approached the table and sat down next to me.

The sun was beaming but it wasn't really a hot day, so I picked a table out on the patio of the café. Fresh air was always relaxing. And with everything going on, I needed relaxation more than ever.

"You're wearing the stress on your face like foundation. What's going on?"

As I prepared to answer, the waitress came to take our orders. "Good afternoon, what can I get for you ladies today?"

"I'll have the Florida Dragon Bowl, and a glass of water please," I replied.

"Let me get the superfood smoothie," Trinity requested.

Once she walked away, I answered, "This unknown number has been calling me, and I don't know if has anything to do with Wallace."

"Have you heard from him?"

"No, the one time I did call him, he didn't answer."

Her doe shaped eyes widened at my response. "Do you think something might've happened to him?" Trinity whispered.

I shook my head. "No, I'm assuming he's laying low for the time being. If I don't hear from him in the next few days I'll reach out to his firm, see if he's been to the office."

The waitress returned with our orders. The second she was out of earshot; we picked our conversation about the situation that Wallace had potentially gotten us both into. There wasn't much I knew about his dealings, but nothing prepared me for the life that he'd thrusted me into. The thought alone was exhausting. After meeting with Trinity, I still had four hours left at work before I could go home to soak in my bathtub.

The waitress returned a while later with the receipt for our bill, but neither of us had given her a card or left the table. "Who paid for it?" I asked.

"I did."

His voice.

His voice was deep and sultry, stirring my heart at the sound massaging my ears. With no rebuttals from the last of my good sense, I turned to stare into the eyes of a man whose voice had the power to seize my being with a glimpse and two words.

Two words.

One touch.

The full beard against his skin, the color of raw honey, sent my mind into overdrive, running wild with thoughts of the many ways I could hydrate it. My eyes danced around his muscular arms decorated with tattoos, not an inch of them untouched was by ink. His thick brows furrowed as he peered down at me.

"Damn," Trinity murmured, freeing me of the trance he'd captivated me in.

"Would you ladies mind if I have a seat?"

Before either of us had the chance to object, he was sitting directly across from me, pulling me into him by the second. He spoke to Trinity while staring at me. "If you don't mind, can I have a moment to speak to your friend?"

She stood to oblige his request as he directed his attention at me, but I grabbed her hand under the table, wordlessly pleading with her to not leave me alone. I was losing control of my senses by the second. Fear of me losing control of them all from being left alone with him was rapidly settling in.

Somehow, I mustered up to the strength to lie. "No, she

can't."

The beautiful creation of a man ran his hand through his beard. "Are you sure you don't want to spend just a moment alone with me?"

Standing up abruptly, I took off in the direction of my car. I felt his eyes on me as I quickened my pace. Sinking into the seat of my car, I pushed a hard exhale from my body, grateful the air was moving through my lungs again. No one person deserved to wield that power over another. That shit was primal. Instinctually, I wanted to give him whatever he requested.

The ringtone blaring from my phone as I tried to reclaim my peace, startled me. Trinity's name across the screen had me quick-swiping trying to answer faster. "Yeah."

"Girl what the hell was that?"

"I don't even know." Resting my head on my steering wheel, it finally hit me how insane I must've looked running away from him.

"I do. A fine ass man wanted to give you some attention and you couldn't figure out how to act because you are walking around with that broken pussy. It needs the dust knocked off."

"What?" The annoyance was rapidly overtaking me.

"You heard me, or did you lose your hearing on your sprint? You are scary as fuck Willow." Trinity's giggling tipped the scales and that was it. I was highly annoyed.

It wasn't as if I was a high school freshman getting approached for the first time. I had boyfriends in the past. Love nor infatuation were new to me. "Bye Trinity, I'll see you later."

"No you won't. I'm going to be at Quan's tonight. You need to go find that nigga that had you running, see if he can turn you into a bedroom track star."

"Bye." I hung up the phone and headed straight to work.

The rest of my day ran together. Typically, work was the perfect distraction. My job was extremely demanding since I was the head software engineer. If we were contracted out, I decided which of the software engineers would be in charge of the account. Still, the time left in my shift dragged by. Since Trinity was going to be with the new beau, I stopped by my favorite sushi spot to grab a quick dinner for the night.

Walking into my house, I felt lighter. The weight I'd been carrying throughout the day was long gone. Hanging my key by the door, I made my way to the living room. I was going to eat my sushi, take a bath, lay up in bed, and watch sappy love movies until I fell asleep. In a way, I was grateful that Trinity was spending the night out. As much as I loved her, I knew she would to go in full detail at how I acted around that man.

How the hell was I supposed to explain something to her that I didn't fully comprehend? With all that I had going on, that was the last thing I wanted to deal with. My cousin meant well but it wasn't what I wanted. I didn't swear men away altogether; they simply weren't my focus. Some men took and gave nothing in return.

I lied.

They easily left you the pieces to a broken heart, and a broken pussy. There was no denying I was a woman scorned. Hell yeah, I was muthafucking bitter. Bitter fucking Betty. Giving your all, in exchange for lies and deceit would bring any woman to her hilt, with no reverence to her strength. Until I put in the work to be healed from that, there was no way in heaven or hell that I would to put that off on the next man. Not when the man that caused it was living his life.

I sat on the couch, savoring both the final bites of the California roll, while Kiana Lede's *Second Chances* blared in the background, drowning out my thoughts of him. Tears spilled down my cheeks as the memories of us battled the lyrics in the song.

You missed out on a blessing, I made you the king of my world

I thought you'd be by my side like you and me saving the world

I- did you think about that

'Bout the time that I'll never get back

No more second chances, chances.

When I was spent from the mix of an aching heart and falling tears, I cleared my face and undressed in the living room. Carrying my clothes, I climbed up the stairs to my bedroom. The pain in my chest was almost unbearable. Even walking was hard, and I hated that I had unearthed this grief again. My deepest desire was to bury it as far down as it would go so I could move on, but something always stopped me. I couldn't.

He wouldn't let me.

Love wouldn't let me.

Even in the darkness I could outline his silhouette. It wasn't necessary to see him, the moment I crossed the threshold of my bedroom I felt him. Though there was no way I truly could, I prepared for our reunion. Flooding the room with light our eyes met, and his name fell from my lips in a faded whisper.

"Grym."

The sweetest word I'd ever tasted.

CHAPTER SIX

Grym

My soul shook at the tremble of her voice.

My spirit sang at the blessing of holding her in my sight, ashamed though, to be met with her tear stained cheeks.

"Willow."

Rising from her bed, I propelled my body towards her, her body repelled, stepping backwards to keep the space between us. "Mama, I miss you."

"You light skin muthafucka! How fucking dare you show up at the café with me and Trinity? What makes you think I would want to be alone with you? The fucking nerve of you to show up at my house, Grym!"

Her anger was justified, but that didn't mean I was going to stand there letting her talk to me however she felt. Willow had one more time to call me a muthafucka. I had been calling from a new number, hoping to speak to her but I froze the minute I heard her voice. After the first, she ignored all my other calls. So I decided to track her down and it wasn't hard to do. My plan to avoid causing a scene by showing up to the café failed, which led to the last-ditch effort of parking my car down the street and breaking into her house.

"Willow, we can talk about this."

"No. Hell no we can't. You made your choice and I made mine." The rage and pain contorted her features as she threw the clothes in her hand at me.

"Mama calm your ass down."

"Fuck you, you light skin muthafucka."

Before she could fully blink, her back was pressed against the door with my face so close my exhales were her inhales. "I let you make it with the first one. Watch your mouth mama."

Even with the tension between us mounting, all I wanted was to run my hands through her curls while I laid kisses to every inch of her chocolate skin. The fire in her eyes betrayed the harsh words and attitude as I watched her battle internally to not give in.

"I'm not scared of you Grym."

I took a couple of steps back. "I never wanted you to be. Can we talk? Please?"

"What more is there for us to talk about?" Willow brushed past me, lifted her clothes from the floor and placed them in the wooden basket in her closet, all while giving me the barest minimum of her attention.

I could have picked anything, asked about her life now. Instead I chose, "Us."

Willow's face twisted up in confusion. "Us? Nigga this

look like a Jordan Peele movie to you? 'Us' ended over a year ago when you lied to me. When you used me!"

I ran my hand down my face as I released a heavy sigh. That wasn't the Willow I had gotten to know. That wasn't the sweet, soft woman I had fallen for two years ago. I had no one to blame but myself. My actions had turned her cold. That shit was eating at me because she was my soft spot. She was the only person that I could take down every wall and not worry about being judged. Until she did and still that was my fault.

"I didn't lie to you. And I sure as hell didn't use you."

"Omitting the truth is the same as lying. Those software hacking skills that you've mastered, did you have to attend a class for that?"

"You have the right…"

"Don't tell me what I have the right to," Willow frothed.

The backlash wasn't unwarranted. I was well aware that I would have to face it at some point in this lifetime. Though it came sooner than I thought, well I'd come sooner than I thought. "Five minutes. That's all I'm asking for."

Willow folded her arms across her plump breasts. My eyes journeyed the length of her body and I felt my focus dwindling as her skin glistened, clad in a lace bra and thong set. Internally I rallied myself to get back to the task at hand. I salivated at the thought of sliding the shit right off her and suffocating between her thighs.

"Two minutes."

Willow and I met when we needed each other the most. I couldn't be convinced of love, let alone at first sight until

I laid eyes on her.

Her beauty was mesmerizing.

Her smile snapped a nigga up in a trance with the quickness.

Her eyes had me looking like a lame nigga gazing into them in the middle of the aisle in Best Buy.

Two years prior, on a trip for a new laptop to help me more with software coding, I left with more than I'd bargained for. I needed the laptop to practice hacking, it was frustrating having to find coders when I came across a system I couldn't hack. When I say Willow, against my better judgement, I asked for her number.

As much as I tried to talk myself out of using it, I was calling her that same day for dinner. Everything with Willow fell together organically. From that day she was under me, and we rarely spent time apart. Our love was unexpected, it came in fast and hard, like a whirlwind. We were warped by passion that devoured any thought of there being someone better.

I made the mistake of asking her about her career as a software engineer. I couldn't lie most of my skills, I'd learned from her. She was nurturing and so naturally giving, I never intended for her to feel used. The day I shared my truth with her, was the day I lost her.

Willow was my rib.

Time and distance had separated us for over a year and she was still my driving force.

She was there when I needed her the most. My soul was gone from the lives that I took and with day I spent with her, she replenished me. I couldn't go any more days without her. I had stayed away long enough and I was ready to be happy again.

I was ready to live again.

I was ready to love again.

"I never used you. It's not like I could've been transparent from the start about what I did for a living. I'm man enough to admit that I should have just let you go. But what I'm not about to let you do is downplay my love for you. When I approached you my intentions were to get to know you. I didn't come looking for you, I didn't even know shit about you or where you worked."

"That doesn't mean you didn't take advantage of me." The gentle soul I'd fallen in love with slowly rose to the surface.

"Mama, I promise I never meant to take advantage of you. I can't change the past but give me a chance to do better now so we can have the future we planned," I pleaded with her.

Willow's arms fell to her side, even her body was tired of fighting me. I had wronged her. All I needed was a chance for her to let me in, I could make it right again. But having Willow bloom for me again was in no way going to be an easy task. "How can I ever trust you?"

Slowly walking over to her, I drew her into my arms. The sensation of her body against mine left me light headed. When she placed her arms around my neck, I knew just what to do. "Where's your bathroom?"

"Down the hallway to the right," she mumbled into my chest.

Picking her up bridal style I carried down the hall. In

the bathroom I sat her on the toilet seat as I lit the candles she had lining her tub. Under the sink, I found her bath bombs and bubble bath. "Which one do you want mama?"

"The pink bath bomb."

I prepared her bath and placed her in the tub. With her eyes closed, head tilted back enjoying the feel of the water, Willow asked, "Why now Grym? Why are you here now?"

Resting on edge of the tub, I offered her the respect of the truth. "I saw you."

Willow's eyes shot open. "When? Where?"

I couldn't meet her questions with honesty, so I avoided answering them. "When you left me, it was the worst pain I've ever been through. A nigga been shot twice and those bullets ain't got shit on you mama," I joked hoping to ease the tension between us.

Watching Willow walk out of my life was the hardest thing I'd ever endured in my thirty-two years. A nigga grew up without a mother and father. I had no family until I met Green. I hadn't experience unconditional love until she came into my life offering it to me naturally. The shit was hard to accept but she didn't give me much of an option. Even with Green, although he was my brother, we understood that our bond was contingent to our loyalty for one another. With Willow, her love for me wasn't attached to anything but who I was as a person. That was something I couldn't forever

Staying away from Willow was much harder. But I owed her that much. I owed her the time to wrap her mind around my chosen profession as the bringer of death. I owed her the space to hate me in hopes she'd choose to show me love me again. The only thing that eased the pain of us being apart was knowing that I would reunite us once again.

The time had come.

She snickered and closed her eyes again. "I hated you."

"I know."

"I love you," she whispered.

My heart beat against my chest like Haitian drums calling me back home. "I love you too mama."

I kissed her forehead, hopeful that we'd be better than before.

CHAPTER SEVEN

Willow

I hated Grym.

Hated him.

Until I saw him…

And the hatred I harnessed evaporated without a trace to hold onto. Seeing him at the café left me frazzled. I didn't want to unravel for him. The woman I was didn't want to be weak for a man who took lives without a second thought. Yet, that was exactly the woman I was. Grym had more power over me than I had over myself. Where love lived, pride could not exist.

He was polished yet rough around the edges. Our up-bringings were different. Though I grew up in Little Haiti, my mother worked hard to provide for us after my father passed away. When she married Wallace, I wasn't as happy as before, but I had a mom that loved and cared for me, and a man that – at least – made an effort to be a role model.

Grym grew up being shuffled from foster home to foster

home until the group home, not ever knowing his parents. He'd told me the only family he had was his brother, though I didn't get a chance to meet him. He went to college to obtain a degree yet he was true to who he was at his core.

In teaching Grym how to love, I learned how to love deeply. Grym pushed me to be better, to be more, and to love harder than I ever loved. A part of me had resented for so long because while we were apart, I couldn't stop my love for him if I wanted to. And trust me, I had prayed that shit away hoping it would stop my longing for him.

His career as an assassin was hard to accept initially. It became easier when he explained the nature of the jobs he accepted. But there was no erasing the damage done when I uncovered that he was using me. I was teaching him because I thought we'd bonded over my love of tech. I felt used, dirty, and like a killer myself when I found out he was using what I taught to eliminate his targets.

I questioned his motives. Had he researched me, could he feel I was lonely when he approached me? I was still grieving the loss of my mother when we met. Was that what attracted him to me? Even though he swore he'd had no clue who I was, my mind then, was too clouded to believe him.

"I hated you." I no longer did.

"I know." Sorrow dripped from Grym's voice.

"I love you." I never stopped.

"I love you too, mama." The relief in his voice was evident.

Two minutes had long come and gone. I didn't want to

talk about the past anymore. If we were going to make something of our reunion, we had ample time to talk through everything. Right now, I needed to feel him.

Grym watched my every move as I glided from the tub to the shower to rinse off. His eyes spilling the thoughts his mouth wouldn't. I fell for him almost immediately in the beginning. There was no way for me to have known I'd meet the love of my life in Best Buy, the day I caved and finally went looking for a new TV.

His long strides propelled him closer to me, authority and confidence weaved in his stance, the hidden softness in his eyes telling the story of a lost boy and I was all in from that moment. He possessed a brooding intensity, choosing to introduce himself with the tale of his birth. Bringer of death because as his mother was taking her last breath, he was taking his first. They named him Grym.

Parts of me felt foolish for being as invested as I was but I received the same in return. Grym was all mine just like I was all his. We opened up to each other, granting access to the parts hidden from the world. He helped me come to terms with my mother's death. No one, not even Trinity was able to do that. A stranger that I had barely known was able to help me heal from my deepest pain. That wasn't something I could take lightly. Our grief and openness to one another is what bonded us in the beginning. We were both craving a love that only the other could provide.

I didn't doubt Grym's love at all, my main concern was trust. Would I be able to grow with him knowing how he made his money? Was I built to endure the fear of him not returning home to me? Even with him sitting in my bathroom I wasn't able to answer those questions. The truth was, I ran at the first sign of trouble. Love should've taken precedence to all of that. That was the internally struggle that was battling with every hour that he was not around to nourish our shared love.

Out of the shower, I wrapped a towel around myself before retiring to my bedroom. Grym followed behind me silently anticipating what I would say or do next. I had so many hidden emotions slowly overwhelming me before I succumbed to numbness. In less than six hours I'd gone from shocked and sad, through anger, and settled on relieved. And it all tied to one man—Grym.

I sat on my queen-sized bed as Grym stood by the door. His hands tucked in the pockets of his sweatpants, waiting for me to say something. Not knowing silence was better than anything I had to say. In the silence we didn't have to worry about saying the wrong things.

I didn't have to bear through his apologies for his secrets and my heartache. There was no excusing using me to master systems hacking.

In the silence I didn't have to admit I desperately wanted to mend our broken hearts. Grym's lies cracked them. I ripped them apart when I ran.

The void, the space between the words, was exactly where we needed to be.

Standing up, I dropped my towel on the carpeted floor. My feet glided me to the man my body craved the most. His manhood stood at attention in the gray sweatpants he wore as my honeycomb pulsed. Before I could make my way toward him, Grym had me in the air with my legs wrapped around him. His lips crashing against mine, connecting our flesh for the first time in over a year.

Grym pressed my back against the wall to support me as he freed himself. In one swift motion, he was all the way inside of me. My honey dripped down his length, guiding him in and out. My moans matched his groans the harder he plummeted into me. Punishing me for everyday he was deprived of my honied nectar.

"Shit you feel good, mama."

I teased him. "You didn't miss this pussy did you Grym?"

"Fuck yeah I missed my pussy," he grunted as he quickened his pace.

Squeezing my pussy muscles around his dick, I held onto him tightly.

"Fuck! Fuck! Fuck! Stop playing with me Willow!" he ordered.

Ignoring him, I released only to tighten my grip again. He pulled out leaving me empty, and I instantly regretted talking shit.

Grym dropped me to my feet and undressed, revealing the masterpiece that was his body. "Get in the bed. Ass up. You talking shit like you don't know wassup. I'm about to eat that pussy 'til you begging me to stop."

I damn near skipped to the bed when he smacked my ass. I assumed the position and knew he wasn't planning to take it easy on me when I felt his large hands spread my ass cheeks apart. We were going to spend the rest of the night making up.

Grym placed a finger in my asshole as he latched onto my clit. I was more than ready for the consequences of my shit talking.

CHAPTER EIGHT

Grym

My vibrating phone woke me up to a reality pulled straight from my dreams. Willow was in my arms after a long night of reuniting. Looking over, I smiled at how peacefully she was sleeping. Everything wasn't fixed between us, but we were off to a good start.

I went to hit ignore on the call but Green's name calling me had me on high alert. "You good G?"

"Code red. I need you at the spot right now."

"Fuck. Give me thirty minutes." For Green to request me at the spot meant the situation was dire. He only called code red, when someone had to be handled.

Having to tell Willow that I had to leave to handle business was the last thing I wanted to do. But I didn't have much of a choice. I brushed her hair out of her face hoping that would be enough to wake her up. It was three in the morning and I needed to leave to handle business. Silently, I prayed it wouldn't blow up in my face.

"Mmmmm. Grym it's swollen. Your dick wouldn't fit the last time remember."

I chuckled. "No mama, I have to go but I'll be back."

Willow slowly opened her eyes. The nightlight that she had to have due to her fear of the dark illuminated the room. "What time is it?"

"It's three in the morning. My brother called…"

"At three in the morning?" Willow's right eyebrow rose as a sign of curiosity.

"Yes."

"You expect me to believe that?"

She had every right to doubt me. I had never deliberately lied to her nor cheated. But in her eyes, not keeping it a hundred had her thinking I was living a double life. "Yes because I'm telling you the truth."

Without saying another word, Willow rolled over, turning her back towards me. Even with me wanting to reassure her, I couldn't. That was only going to lead to her asking me questions that I didn't want to answer. Although she was aware of what I was doing a year ago, I was going to find a better time to inform her that I was still doing it.

Not to mention I still planned on killing Wallace. Through my research, I found out he was her stepfather. She had spoken of him without ever mentioning his name during our seven-month relationship, but I had never gotten the chance to meet him. The two weren't close from what I could recall of our conversations about him. I was hoping it was still that way because Wallace had an expiration date and it was fast approaching.

"I'll be back, I promise mama." Getting out of the bed, I picked my clothes up from the floor. Once I was fully dressed, I kissed her on her lips and said good bye. She gave me the cold shoulder but that was expected. When I came back it would be a different story.

When I made it outside, I jogged down the street to where my parked car was located. Green called me as soon as I drove off. "I'm on the way."

"You finally got some pussy last night?"

"Nigga what?" I pulled the phone away from ear to stare at the screen. When I saw that it was in fact Green, I placed it back.

"I can hear it in your voice man. A nigga thought he did earlier, but I wasn't sure. I called back to make sure." His goofy ass laugh that followed made me hang up on him. My mood wasn't right to deal with Green's dumbass antics.

When I made it to the spot, I pulled my .45 out of my glove compartment. It was my favorite piece to carry regularly. After parking, I walked up to the porch to find Green smoking a blunt.

"Hell yeah. You got the 'I got some pussy' look all over your light skin face."

Green was as light skin as I was, and he had green eyes which was how he got the name. "Nigga fuck you."

"What broad finally has you loosening up? Don't tell me it's Nikki from the cookout. I saw how her ratchet ass was looking at you." His deep laughter made me want to punch his ass right in his throat.

"Nigga don't you ever disrespect me like that or I'm going

to shoot your ass. No cap. Where's the code red?"

Green took a buff his blunt and threw his hands up in surrender. "We have two problems, but one can wait for later."

"What's going on?"

"Word is that Marco has been running his mouth and touching what isn't his."

"Tell me more."

Marco was one of his most loyal soldiers. Before I walked away from the drug game, I was the one that brought him on. I was basically training him to be Green's right hand since I was stepping down. If the information that Green had was valid, then he did right by calling me. I had to be the one to pull the trigger.

"I've been kicking it with Tasha a bit. So earlier tonight when I went to her apartment, she was acting off a bit. We smoked a blunt, she topped me off, and I was ready to get the fuck out of there."

I shook my head at him fucking with Tasha. It wasn't the fact that she was loose with her body that bothered me. A woman's value didn't decrease by how many dicks she sucked or fucked. It was determined based on how she viewed herself. If she viewed herself as a hoe than that was her call. What I didn't like was the dishonesty. If you were tricking off for a come up, then say that was what the fuck you wanted. I had more respect for that than a woman that was acting loyal to a nigga but fucking off with other niggas for a few dollars. That shit didn't sit well with me. Tasha was a snake. I saw the shit from a mile away.

Green continued, "When I was getting ready to leave, that's when she started to really move funny. She was doing everything to keep me there. She even offered to call up her friend Nikki for a threesome."

I listened tentatively trying to gauge in what direction the story was going. Green being as relaxed as he was a sign that the situation was handled for the most part. "Nigga, get to the point."

"It's call building the climax nigga. That's an important part of being a storyteller."

"Bruh you a fucking drug dealer. Fuck out of here with that story telling shit." He clearly wasn't pressed for time.

He chuckled. "My bad, the loud is hitting. Once Tasha said that shit, I pulled my gun out on her. She started singing like a fucking bird. Tasha was supposed to keep me from the trap house so Marco could run the shit. Where jit messed up was thinking I'd put pussy above my money. Only clown niggas did that shit and last time I checked, I ain't ever been to a circus a day in my life."

Jit was a Miami slang for the young gangstas. Jit had fucked up big time thinking the way he did. Pussy never came before money. A wife, now that was a different story. "What proof did Tasha have?"

"She recorded her conversation with Marco as insurance that he wouldn't hurt her. Nikki knew about it but was too scary to participate. Tasha got scared, showed it to me thinking I'd protect her."

"Where is she at now?"

A mischievous grin appeared on his face. "Tied up in the

trunk waiting for the Grym Reaper. Marco is at home thinking shit is sweet."

"Say less."

For Green to think I was off, he was riding around with a body of someone he was involved with in his trunk. To cover his tracks, he texted Nikki from Tasha's phone that he never showed up to her house and that she was going to go visit Marco. He turned her phone off at her house and that gave me the perfect set up.

"I already know how I'm going to handle it. I hate that I have to ask you this, but did you nut in that girl's mouth?"

"Her dry ass mouth couldn't even get me off, nigga." A look of disappointment appeared on his face.

Green was ignorant as fuck, but he was an honest nigga. I couldn't do nothing but respect that. We left the spot and went to my house to drop my car off. After that, we had to go to Tasha's for me to retrieve Green's car and headed directly to Marco's house. It was crazy to think that I was breaking bread with him the other only to have to end his life the next. That was how life worked though. Greed was a muthafucka and Marco was minutes from finding how much.

By the time we had gotten there it was well into four in the morning. Circling the block, we saw Marco's car was the only one in the drive way. I had Green park down the street away from any lights and I parked behind him. Getting out of my car, I went to Tasha's trunk to pull her out the car but what I saw stopped me right in my tracks.

The nigga had her tied up like a pig with an actual apple in her mouth.

Shaking my head, I was unable to hold in the laughter that escaped my throat. "You a sick muthafucka you know that Green?"

"Says the nigga that thinks its comical," he rebutted.

Ignoring him, I turned my attention to Tasha. "Here's what's going to happen, I'm going to take you out the car. First thing you're going to do is turn your phone back on. Next, you're going to take your shirt off to wipe down car inside and out. When you're done, put it back on and Green is going to get in the car with you while I wait in the bushes outside of Marco's house. If you try some funny shit, Green will kill your ass without any hesitation. Nod to show me you understand."

Tears streamed down her face which didn't move me. She got herself in a situation that she shouldn't have been in. That wasn't on me, and I sure as hell wasn't going to lose any sleep over it either.

I continued, "Once you're done, you're going to tell Marco you're outside his house and for him to come to the door. You do that and I won't kill you. Nod if you understand."

She nodded bringing us to an agreement. Retrieving my black leather gloves from my pockets, I quickly slipped them on. Untying Tasha, I removed her from the trunk of her own car. I took the apple out of her mouth and handed it to Green to put in his pocket.

Tasha did exactly as she was instructed to do. It only took one ring for Marco to rush down the stairs to open the door wearing a terry robe. We hid off to side of the door so that he would only be able to see her when he opened up. The second she was in the door, Green and I pushed in behind her.

The color from Marco's face drained from his face at the sight of Green and I in his living room with our guns drawn. "Yo what's going on?"

"Take that base out your voice before I knock it out bitch," I grunted.

"Nikki is here," Tasha whispered.

"How you know?" Green asked.

"That's her purse right there." She pointed at a small black leather purse on the couch.

The perfect idea popped in my head. We were about to get rid of all the loose ends.

"Let's take this the bedroom, shall we?" Walking up to Marco, I pressed my gun to his right temple. "Lead the way nigga."

Marco did as I said. Green followed behind Tasha with his gun glued her back. Marco opened his bedroom door to reveal Nikki's nasty ass butt naked in his bed. When she saw that we were all there, she tried to cover up however it was too late. I had seen some shit that had me swallowing my vomit.

Tasha was fighting hard to fight her tears while Nikki was letting that shit flow freely. Green spoke first, "Jit I thought you was real."

"I am man. What's going on? What's this about?" Marco's voice began to shake as fear began to take over him.

"This about you scheming and taking from me. Don't lie or I'll shoot you dead right here."

"I'm sorry bro. Please, I'm begging you. I'll pay you back

with interest. Put me back on the block. Whatever I got to do to make this right, I'll do." Marco pleaded with Green.

I would've had more respect if he took the shit like a man. He thought he was king when he was stealing. Now that his life was seconds from ending, he wanted to beg like the bitch that he was.

"What you think Grym?" Green knew this was like game-day to me. I already had the vision in my head.

"Where's your strap at?" I asked Marco.

"I don't have one in here," he lied.

He was a simp so I was positive he had it hidden in the most obvious place. "Tasha snatch the lamp and throw it at this nigga's head for lying to me."

Tasha moved so quick, all I saw was the lamp flying and smashing on Marco's head. He grabbed the side of his head but didn't utter a sound.

"Tasha you follow instructions and I like that." She smiled at me thinking that I was leading her closer to freedom. "Nikki y'all was about to fuck right?"

Nikki wiped away her tears and nodded. "Yeah."

"Alright Marco, go ahead and fuck her."

He looked around the room confusingly. "I don't understand."

"What part of fuck Nikki don't you comprehend. Stick your limp dick inside her fishy ass pussy," Green instructed. That nigga was getting more foolish by the minute.

When he didn't move, I told Tasha to slap and scratch

him. She ran up on that man like she was Floyd Mayweather punching him and scratching the fuck out of him. She was fighting to save her life not knowing that she was only creating the perfect crime scene. Marco pushed her off and she went stumbling back.

"You know what? Never mind. Tasha go in his nightstand and pull out his strap," I demanded. Just like I thought she would, she hurriedly went in there and pulled his piece out. That nigga was a simp.

"Man, if you're going to kill me just kill me."

"Oh you're going to die nigga, you don't even have to ask. Tasha, shoot that nigga. It's your life or his."

Her hands shook but she sent two bullets ripping into Marco's chest. Blood spewed from his chest as he fell to the floor. Without me having to instruct her, she turned the gun to Nikki and did the same. That's what fear did. It had the possibility of making you turn on those that you were supposed to be most loyal to.

"Can I go now please? I promise I won't say anything."

"How can I trust you when you just killed your best friend?" I asked.

"But y'all..." she started.

G cut her off, "We didn't tell you to kill Nikki. You did that all on your own."

Marco lived in the hood therefore the cops weren't going to be called right away. By the next round of gunshots, someone might've, and I wasn't trying to take any chances.

"You said you weren't going to kill me." Her voice cracked, as her legs buckled under her and she fell to the ground. She had a loaded gun in her hand, yet fear had paralyzed her causing her to lose her fight reflex. Walking over to her, I grabbed her hand to help her place the gun at her right temple.

"I'm not. You're going to kill yourself. Tonight, you met the Grym Reaper."

Tasha's hand quivered as she pulled the trigger ending her own life. Whether I pulled the trigger or not, she was a dead woman. She understood that. Tasha chose to end her life on her own terms. She made my plan to orchestrate a murder-suicide go off without a hitch. I didn't mind getting my hands dirty but when shit played out that way, it made things a lot easier.

The second we confirmed that all three were dead, Green and I got the hell up out of there. I was exhausted but I had to get back to Willow. I got in the driver's seat and pulled away heading to Green's house to get my car. On the way, I called Willow five times with no response.

"You ready for number two?" Green asked from the passenger seat.

Whether I was ready or not, I had to find out. "What is it?"

"Santino ordered off the hit on Wallace for now." Santino didn't offer Green any other explanation than he wanted to wait it out, see if there was a different manner it could be handled in

That shit bothered me. Something was up but it wasn't up to me to find out what it was. I urged Green to keep his eyes and ears open for any information. A muthafucka didn't stop wanting a nigga dead out of nowhere.

One thing was for sure, it was no longer a secret I was

keeping from Willow. Santino changing his mind gave me the opportunity to solely focus on repairing things with her. Taking my phone out of my pocket, I dialed her number again. When it didn't ring, I called back five more times. Still wasn't ringing. Willow had blocked my damn number. She had me fucked up.

Hopping on the highway, I sped up I-95. Originally, I was going to drop Green off and get my car to head back to Fort Lauderdale. But with her blocking my number, I had to change things ASAP.

"Where the hell you going nigga? This ain't the way to my house," Green stated

"We going to Fort Lauderdale. I got to handle something."

Willow had me all the way fucked up.

CHAPTER NINE

Willow

Grym had me fucked up.

If he thought it was okay for him to leave my bed at three in the morning, he had another thing coming. Though we had been apart over a year, I knew that Grym would've never left my bed to be with another woman. It was the thought of him leaving me to go take someone's life that troubled me.

The minute he left, I blocked his number. When sleep couldn't be persuaded to stay, I called Trinity asking her to come home. She didn't ask any questions when I called but we both knew she'd have a hundred by the time I brought her up to speed. There were going to be aspects of Grym's life that I couldn't divulge to her, which was okay. The most important parts, I would be able to spill freely over a cup of hot chocolate.

"Y'all been broken up for over a year and he just showed up last night after seeing you out?"

"Yes," I replied. Trinity had posed that same question at every point in our twenty-minute conversation.

"What kind of magic do you have in your pussy to have a nigga breaking into our house in the middle of the day after seeing you once after a year, Willow?"

I rolled my eyes while taking a sip of my hot cocoa. "Trinity I'm for real."

"Shit me too. You ran away from this man and a year later, you're sitting on his face."

"It's not the sex." It was way more than the sex. It was having your soulmate near for the first time in what seemed like eternity. No matter how mad I was at Grym, love was our constant.

"I know it isn't but damn. What are you going to do?"

That was a question that I had no idea how to answer. "I blocked his number. That's all I got so far."

The confused expression on Trinity's face told me what I said didn't make sense to her. "Willow, this nigga broke into our house. What the hell do you think blocking his number is going to do?" She began to laugh hysterically before she continued, "I'll tell you. It won't do a damn thing."

No sooner than the last word escaped Trinity's mouth, we turned around to the sound of keys unlocking our front door. The door sung open and there stood Grym along with the light bright nigga with green eyes. The look on his Grym's face was menacing. The softness that was usually displayed in his eyes was replaced with anger.

They entered the house as if they owned it. Walking over, they sat on the other side of the sectional that Trinity and I were sharing. "Did these niggas just walk into our house like they own it?" Trinity's eyes kept hopping from me to them.

"Niggas? Don't refer to your future husband as a nigga baby," the man with the green eyes said.

"Future husband?" Trinity and I questioned simultaneously.

"Yes. I'm your future husband baby. My name is Green, but you can call me daddy." That nigga might've lacked something but it sure as hell wasn't confidence.

"Nigga that little ass dick you packing couldn't make a virgin call you daddy," Trinity quipped.

"Ignore him. Willow, can I speak with you in private?" Grym interjected.

I was kind of afraid to leave Trinity alone with Green because she would eat him alive. I was even more terrified to be alone with Grym. Against my better judgment, I had him follow me upstairs to my room.

Entering the bedroom last, Grym closed the door behind us. He was in my face and had me up against a wall within seconds. "Blocking my number. That's how want to do this mama?"

His chest rose up and down as it filled with anger. Looking up in his eyes, I saw that the softness had returned welcoming me home. "When did you make a key to my house?"

"I took yours on my way out."

"So you're not only a murderer and a liar. You're a thief as well. Got it."

And that quickly the anger returned. Grym pinched the

brim of his nose as he began to speak. "I'm going to let you have that one but trust, it will be the last one. I stayed away for as long as I could because you deserved that space to process what you learned about me. What you have to understand is there is no more running away."

He paused and continued, "There are no more breaks. Ain't going to be no more blocking my number. We are going to sit here and talk this shit out. If you feel as though you have to punch me, do that shit. Whatever questions you have, I will answer the best way I can. We are going to fix this because I'm not going another day without my heart."

My weak attempt of shoving him away did nothing to move him. My hands stayed glued to his hard chest. Love shouldn't have to be as difficult as this was. The complexity intertwined with the simplicity of it, made love the most beautiful contradiction to ever exist.

Grym took a tight hold of my wrists. "Willow we have to talk this out. If you can tell me to my face that we're done, I'll leave right now and never bother you again."

I buried my head in his chest hoping to draw some of his courage. "I can't do that."

He let go of my wrists and lifted me. Carrying me over to the bed, he sat me at the edge of it and kneeled in front of me. "Ask me whatever it is you have to ask for us to move forward. Tell me what you need from me to make sure you have security in us, mama."

"Why did you lie about what you did for a living?"

"I do have investments in tech companies as well as real-estate. As far as my other profession, me not telling you had to do less with me not trusting you and more to do with me protecting you. If you aren't knowledgeable about my dealings the less likely you are to get implicated. I swear there were many times I tried to tell you, but couldn't." The sincerity in his voice wrapped around me giving me the security that I had been longing for.

"Why do you do it?"

He took a deep breath then explained the first time he took a life, he was saving Green's. The streets gave him a family thus he did whatever he had to do to protect that family. He started off selling drugs but quickly realized that the drug dealing life wasn't for him. When he saved Green's life, he felt as though he found his purpose. With each life he took, it became easier to take another. That coupled with how much money he was making from it kept him going.

He had never felt any emotions when taking a life, therefore there was no guilt hindering him from doing his job. It was a means to an end, until it became a part of him. It was a part of him that brought him because he had found something to hold on to. He then elaborated on how he was selective on who his victims were. They had to have been guilty of something in his eyes that warranted death. It wasn't for me to agree with, but I understood it. I was grateful that he opened up.

"When you left at three this morning was it to kill someone?"

Grym closed his eyes and pinched the brim of his nose. "Yes but I didn't kill anyone. Willow, you can't ask me stuff like that. Don't put me in a position to lie to you. If it comes to protecting you, I'll lie to God himself."

I giggled at his effort to lighten up the mood. "Are you ever going to quit?"

"Yes. The plan was always for me to retire at thirty-five. To keep it real with you, I've done it for so long, that it became who I was—the Grym Reaper. I that it would always be that way until I met you. You're the only part of me that is irreplaceable mama."

Afraid to ask him would he stopped sooner I remained silent until he spoke. "Do you view me as a monster?"

"No. You're a good person with a good heart. Your name being Grym doesn't support that though," I said jokingly.

He chuckled, "Yeah, I know."

I continued, "You do bad things but you aren't a bad person. If you were, you'd be incapable of loving me. You love harder than anyone I know. It was never you love that I doubted Grym. It was my ability to trust you."

"I'm going to do whatever it takes to work on that. Can you promise to try with me?"

If he was going to put in the effort to gain my trust, then I was going to love him through it, He went most of his life without love, looking in his eyes, I saw how desperately he needed it.

How desperately we both needed it. "Yes, I promise."

Grym smiled widely, "Now, can I eat my pussy for breakfast?"

"You don't even have to ask." I spread my legs since he was already in the perfect position. Laying back, I rode the wave of ecstasy as he feasted on my yoni.

I was riding for Grym.

I was riding for love.

CHAPTER TEN

Grym

For the past couple of days, I had been doing everything in my power to ensure that Willow and I were on the same page. We had barely touched the surface of the stuff that could negatively impact our relationship. She claimed to be on board but realistically, she was going to have problems accepting the side of me she didn't know. That part of me was hidden from her intentionally because she deserved more than what the rest of the world was getting from me.

What I didn't want to happen was a repeat of me having to leave to take care of a situation then being bombarded by a hundred questions I couldn't answer. That was why I planned to have a real discussion about us. Willow was my past, present, and without a doubt in my mind, she was my future.

Santino temporarily putting off the hit on Wallace was a curse disguised as a blessing. I would've much rather killed that nigga while Willow and I weren't on the best of terms than to wait until I had to be the one to help her through her grief.

A grief that I would've been the one to cause.

"Having to replace Marco isn't going to be easy," Green blurted, pulling me out of my thoughts. We were at his house to discuss how he was going to shake up his team.

Rumor on the street was that Tasha caught him and Nikki together and lost her mind. The police ruled it a murder suicide like I expected. The messages that Green had sent from Tasha's phone corroborated the story. The detectives didn't know who Green was to find him to question him. Nobody in the hood was going to snitch either. That shit was the least of my worries. However, Green having to replace Marco was a concern.

With Marco being his most trusted worker, to find out that the nigga was scheming was fucked up. It had Green looking at all the other niggas on his team crazy. Someone else had to have known what Marco was up to.

"We should've asked that nigga who was working with him," G continued.

I shook my head. "This is why you're the kingpin and I'm the killer."

"Fuck is that supposed to mean?" Green's chest puffed up, awaiting my answer.

"It means that you can't ever trust a muthafucka whose life you have in your hands nigga."

Marco had already proved himself to be a disloyal and a thief. No information he could've given to us would've been of value. If that nigga could steal from the man that gave him everything, he was sure as hell going to lie to our faces if he thought it was going to save his life.

"You have a point," Marco agreed. "The shit is wild to me. Business has to go on as usual but I dead ass don't trust any of those niggas."

"Green this drug game is like chess nigga. Can't no nigga outplay you in chess and they damn sure ain't about to beat you at this shit. You know exactly what you need to do. You know who's shaky. Handle that shit accordingly. Whatever you need from me, I got you."

The grin on Green's face was sign that he was about to be on some bullshit. "Whatever I need?"

"Why the fuck are you smiling like that nigga?"

"I want Trinity," he announced.

"Nigga hell nah. You not about to have Willow coming at me for you doing her cousin dirty. I'm still working on making sure she doesn't up and leave me again. Not to mention that I'm waiting on word to kill her stepfather. You think I'm really about to have you playing with her cousin's emotions to add to that list. Fuck no."

The smile he had quickly turned into a scowl. "Damn you acting like I'm some type of trash nigga or something."

"No, I'm telling you I know you do trash shit. Green I've never seen you be with one woman. Nigga you've never had a serious relationship. Ever. Not one G."

"This is different."

"How?"

Green was a good dude, nevertheless I knew how he was. He lacked love the same way I did having grown up in the system. The shit we saw was our norm and until we saw something new, we fell into the same shit everybody else was doing. Willow was mine and it seemed as though he wanted Trinity to be his. Couldn't admit that I wasn't skeptical.

Most of the time he did mess around with women that didn't have any potential of being more that a fuck off for a couple of weeks. However, I witnessed him first hand turn a couple of great quality women into women scorned. He was my brother, but Willow was not about to blame me if he fucked around on Trinity.

"Trinity ain't tripping off me. When I saw her, I saw my future Grym, no bullshit. She's mean as hell and I love that shit. Before y'all went upstairs, she was trying to play like didn't want a nigga."

"I don't think she was playing fam."

"That's what you think. Look, this is what I need you to do. We just going to pop up over there, we'll cook them dinner or some shit while they're at work. Women never say no to food."

Green must've been feeling Trinity heavy, yet I was leery to go along with his plan. "You want us to break into their house to trick Trinity into having dinner with you?"

"Nigga you acting like you didn't just break into their house the other day."

I couldn't even argue with his logic. Willow and I had been doing good but the second she switched up on me for something, I was going to be at her spot waiting on her. She refused to give me a key which I wasn't even upset about. Willow made it clear that she was all in, but it was going to take more than a few words and actions for her to trust me fully.

"Fine, I got you. Don't make me regret that shit either."

"You got my word nigga. Speaking of word, I got word from Santino."

"What did he say?"

"He said in three weeks' time, he wants you to make the kill."

That shit was suspect as hell. My gut was telling me that Santino was up to something. Green felt the same way I did. For him to be as passionate as he was when I first met him to him now wanting to wait three weeks for the kill, it didn't add up.

Rubbing my hand down my head, I contemplated all of the possibilities for the holdup. The why of the delay. The first time, it was my fuck up. Willow had shown up at Wallace's apartment out of the blue. When I was ready to make the kill, Santino had put it on hold. Now he was requesting that I wait three weeks. If there was a time for me to back out, then it would be it. The problem was that I had already given my word. My word was my bond, I couldn't break that shit. But with how Santino was moving, I didn't trust that shit either.

"I don't like how that nigga is moving G. Something is up. Ain't shit changed about his nephew's situation. That nigga is still going to prison while Wallace is still living life as usual." Because I hadn't gone back on my word of taking Wallace out, I was still tailing him.

"That's the vibe I'm getting too. What you want to do man?"

"I'm torn as hell right now man."

"I can understand why you're second guessing offing Wallace based on how Santino is moving. But why are you torn?" Green asked with his eyes squinting at me.

After the night I dragged Green to Willow's house, I explained to him that Willow was a woman from my past. The one detail I left out was that she was Wallace's stepdaughter, and that Willow was the *she* that showed up at Wallace's apartment the day I went to make the hit.

"Willow is Wallace's daughter."

"Nigga what? Willow is chocolate as hell. Ain't no drop of white in that girl."

His serious tone made me laugh. "He's her step-father."

"And you didn't know this at first."

"Hell nah, man. Seeing her at his condo fucked with me."

When Willow and I got together we were completely engulfed in our relationship. It seemed too good to be true. We wanted to protect our love from the world. She and I opened up to each other, but we agreed to not get others involved hoping to preserve our love from the outside factors that could taint it.

All of our days were spent together.

All of our nights were spent with me inside of her.

Willow was my stillness in the midst of chaos.

We were safe in the bubble that our love had created. While I thought I was protecting us, I was setting myself up to lose her. If I wouldn't have kept us in that bubble I would've probably never been in the position of agreeing to take her step-father from the face of the earth. He may not have been the best to her but then again, he was all she knew.

Green sat up to give me his undivided attention. "You

can't kill him, Grym."

"Yeah I can."

"Let me rephrase that since you didn't get what the point I was trying to make. Yes, you are capable of killing him. You just shouldn't kill him."

"I already agreed to the job. I gave my word nigga. You better than anyone knows how it goes."

"Yeah, you also gave your word to Willow, too. I can give you my opinion all day but it's up to you to make the better decision."

I did give Willow my word to never betray her trust.

I did make a vow to her.

Once again my profession was getting in the way, and this time I had to make a choice that wouldn't end in Willow leaving me.

CHAPTER ELEVEN

Willow

"For some reason I'm extremely annoyed right now," I said to Trinity. We were seated on the patio of a restaurant in downtown Fort Lauderdale, waiting on my stepfather to show up.

For days I tried reaching out to him. My calls and texts would go unanswered. Not once did he bother to contact me back until earlier in the day. The annoyance stemmed from him demanding I fake my death and then falling off the face of the earth. Then out of the blue he requested that we meet for dinner. What he didn't know was that I had no plans of breaking bread with him.

"I know but just hear him out. Maybe he has a good explanation for his actions," Trinity attempted to reason with me. She was the most rational, yet skeptical person I had ever come across.

Right as I went to respond, Wallace came trekking towards us. He wore a pair of sunglasses hiding his eyes. "Sorry, I am late. I was tied up in some business."

"That's fine. You remember my cousin Trinity."

"Yes, how are you?" he directed his question to my cousin.

"Well. Thank you for asking."

"That's good to hear. I won't keep you all long."

The waitress came to get our drink orders interrupting our conversation. Trinity and I ordered an appetizer to share. Saturdays were our pizza night therefore we didn't want to get full. It didn't take long for her to return with our crab cakes and water for the table. We thanked her and she disappeared promising to come back to check on us.

"So what's going on? I've been calling you for days."

"Willow, sweetie, I apologize for my disappearance. This situation is a lot for me to deal with. Which I can understand it is hard for you as well."

Wallace had no clue how hard it was for me. Here I was trying to live my life as normal as possible when it was everything but. He was asking me to fake my death yet wouldn't give me any details other than someone was possibly after him. For all I knew, he could've been talking Casper the ghost.

Not to mention my relationship with Grym. He was putting real effort into ensuring I was secure in us. I was uncomfortable with his life choices but regardless of his side profession, Grym was a good-hearted person. Life handed him a bad hand and he did what it took to survive. Telling Grym what was going on with Wallace would force him to be involved in a situation that would result in someone's life ending. I couldn't be the reason for him having blood on his hands.

"Can you offer me any updates?"

"I'm sorry, Willow. The best option is still for you to leave town by faking your death. It's the only thing that can keep anyone from coming for you."

Without saying another word, Wallace stood up leaving me and Trinity at the table. Looking down, she had eaten all eight of the crab cakes. "For real Trinity? What the hell did you do? Inhale the whole damn plate at once?"

She shrugged her shoulders. "It was either that or curse Wallace's ass out. I get that he's trying to protect you, but the nigga could give you something to go off of. I mean, he could at least tell you how much trouble his stupid ass is in."

The waitress came back to check on us. I gave her my card to pay and once she returned, we headed home. The second we were in the car, Trinity was back talking about the predicament that Wallace had me in. "You should tell Grym."

My heart threatened to leap out of my chest at her declaration. "I can't do that."

"The hell you can't. He's the muthafucking Grym Reaper."

I swerved my car to park on the right shoulder of the interstate trying to understand how Trinity knew Grym's true identity. "What?"

"Willow, we ran in different circles in Little Haiti. I ran with hood niggas while you were in school getting those awards and diplomas. You don't think I know who the hell Green is? I knew who that light bright nigga was the second he stepped foot in the door. As far as Grym, I put one and two together when he showed up with that goofy ass green eyed nigga."

Trinity hadn't thought about leaving Little Haiti until she enrolled cosmetology school. She always made it a point to keep me away from the lifestyle she had submerged herself in whenever I came to visit. As she got older, the further away she strayed from it. After receiving her cosmetology license and her associates in business, she opened up her first salon in Fort Lauderdale and never looked back. After I packed up and moved from Miami, I ran straight to her.

"Speaking of Green why are you so hard on him? I think he really likes you." There was no denying that Trinity had Green's nose wide open. The more she pushed him away, the more she was pulling him in. The more she belittled him her words, the more confidence that nigga had. There was no logical explanation for it.

"Willow, Green is a friendly ass nigga with community dick. Ain't no nigga of mine about to have me out here looking crazy because he lacks self-control. Nope, I can't do it. That nigga would have to eat my pussy every night for a year in order for me to even consider giving him a chance to take me on a date."

Laughing at how serious she was, I went to pull back into traffic, but she stopped me. "Don't try to deflect though. You need to tell Grym."

"I can't tell him."

"Why the fuck not?"

"There's no way I can have that on my conscience. Finding out he killed people for a living was the reason I left him the first time around. Now you want me to practically send him out there to kill someone on my behalf. I wouldn't be able to live with that."

"Why are you with Grym?"

"Because I love him."

"Did you love him a year ago?"

My eyes narrowed in on Trinity, trying to figure out the path that she was leading me down. "Yes."

"Yet you ran from him. You left the city to be away from him. Love isn't why you're with him. Forget being honest with me, Willow. Be honest with yourself." She poked at my chest with her pointer finger.

"I've accepted him."

"There we go. I can't tell you what to do but if you're going to be with a man like Grym, you have to let him be who he is. That man will go to the lengths of the earth for you. Shit he done already broke into our house. All I'm saying is, Wallace got you in this mess and isn't offering any real solutions. Grym would handle it for you."

As much as I hated to admit it, Trinity was right. Love was what bonded but accepting each other was going to be what bonded Grym and I forever.

Wallace had put me in a situation that I had no clue how to handle. His actions had put my life in danger, and he was only offering one solution that didn't make any sense. If anyone could help me figure it out, Grym could.

I had to tell him what was going on.

"I'll call him when we get home."

Getting back on the interstate, we made it home within

five minutes. The first thing I noticed was that the lights were on through the windows. I was certain we'd turned them off when we left earlier in the day. There weren't any cars that we recognized parked near our house. Grym had texted me to let me know he had something come up, and would be over later on in the night after he was done. Which meant it couldn't have been him. He would've called me if there was a change of plans.

With the both of us on high alert, we retrieved our purses and carried them in front of us as we got out the car. As we approached the door, I nodded for Trinity to wiggle the door knob. It being unlocked had our nerves bad especially after our meeting with Wallace. Could everything he had been saying about to play out the second we opened the door?

After sharing a knowing look, Trinity turned the knob and swung the door open to meet whatever our fate was.

CHAPTER TWELVE

Grym

Staring down the barrel of two .22s I didn't know whether to laugh or be proud.

"The next time y'all pull guns make sure you pull the trigger immediately or at least get some shit that can actually do damage." Walking over to Willow, I removed the gun from her hand and kissed the top of her forehead.

"Baby, what are you doing here? You scared the hell out of us."

To better plan the surprise Green needed help setting up, I told Willow I'd be busy. She and Trinity usually had their pizza night thing so it wouldn't bother her as much if something came up. While they were away from the house, Green and I broke in, made them dinner, and set up game night.

"If you would give me a key, I wouldn't have to break in." I could've easily made a copy of her key, but I wanted her to give it to me willingly.

"Y'all niggas crazy as hell," Trinity interjected as she

slipped her gun back into her purse.

"Crazy for you baby," Green added while coming out of the kitchen.

Trinity rolled her eyes as she walked right past him into the kitchen. She could play all she wanted but we could see she was playing hard to get. I couldn't blame her. Green had a reputation that made it hard for any serious woman to take him seriously. I had to hand it to him though, I had never seen the nigga go as hard for a woman as he was going for Trinity. For him to go out of his way to cook anything was beyond me. That nigga didn't even cook for himself.

"Grym you can't keep breaking in here," Willow said.

"Why not?"

"What if you get caught?"

Green's laughter caught both of our attention. "My bad. You were serious?"

"Yes I was serious."

Gliding my head over my waves, I licked my lips. "Give me a key then."

"The only way you're getting a key to this house is if you can guarantee that this clown is not going to show up using it." Trinity returned from the kitchen with a plate of spaghetti that G had prepared and a bottle of ranch in her hand. She sat on the couch eating her food as if she didn't just disrespect Green. Looking at Green, I recognized that he didn't have much patience left in him.

Just like I thought he would, Green walked over and snatched the plate out of Trinity's hand. Willow and I stood silently watching the scene unfold in front of us.

Trinity still had the fork in her hand as she sat on the couch in shock by Green's actions.

"Nigga did you just snatch my plate out of my hand?"

"Yeah and you're not about to do shit about it. I like you Trinity but you're not about to play me like some random ass nigga."

"I'm treating you like the nigga you are, Green. You're for everybody."

"That's where you wrong. I'm trying to be for you, and you alone. I don't cook for everybody but we was in the kitchen cooking for y'all. If you don't want me, say that shit. But this stupid ass game you're playing is dead." With the plate in hand, Green walked into the kitchen, and threw the whole thing in the trashcan. Trinity stood and moved swiftly to join Green in the kitchen.

I couldn't help but laugh at his antics. We were both doing shit outside of the norm. I understood his frustration. Willow tried that playing hard shit with me, and it drove me crazy. The difference between Green and I was, I knew how to handle Willow. He'd yet to figure out Trinity's game plan.

"Are you going to say something to Green," Willow asked me.

"That shit doesn't concern us. Trinity wants to talk to him crazy then he's going to talk to her crazy."

"Grym…"

"Willow trust me. Green ain't going to hurt your cousin. She just needs to soften up some to give him a chance."

Initially, I was against Green going after Willow but the more I saw how he was acting, the more I started to believe that he was serious about her. He had taken a lot of disrespect from Trinity which was hard as hell for him to do.

Seeing as the plans for the night had went down the drain, I came up with an idea to give us all some alone time. "Let's go."

"Where are we going?"

"You ask way too many questions mama." Pulling my phone out, I did what I had to before stuffing it back into my pocket.

With her hand in mine, I led Willow to my car that was parked down the street. Since Green was dead set on us making it a surprise, he suggested that we parked the car away from their house. If he and Trinity weren't two crazy muthafuckas, the night would've gone as planned.

First, I stopped by her favorite sushi spot to pick up our orders. Afterwards, I drove to a near by park. When we made it, I went into my trunk to retrieve a blanket.

"Oh my goodness baby. You still have that blanket."

"Of course I do." Willow wrapped her arms around my waist and rested her head against my chest. I kissed the top of her head full of hair, reminiscing on how much she had changed me.

She'd shown me how to show love.

When Willow and I first began dating I had never kissed a woman. That shit was way too intimate for the women that I was dealing with. Dates weren't something that I ever did. Shit I barely even communicated with women when we were apart. That all changed the moment she and I got involved. Willow was all about romance and since I was all about her, I became all about romance.

Her touches eased my spirit.

Her kisses replenished my soul.

Her love gave me a reason to live.

Within our seven-month relationship, I acquired the skill of consistency. I was planning dates and surprising her with the small things that would bring a smile to her gorgeous chocolate face. My hands couldn't stay off of her. She shown me that love was more than a simple word.

Love was an action.

Love was a commitment.

Love was taught to me by the only woman that had ever been deserving of mine.

As the sun was setting, I laid her favorite throw blanket out on the grass. I had purchased it for our third date and kept in my trunk for whenever she wanted to have an impromptu picnic in the park. Willow loved all that sappy shit. And because I loved the shit out of her, I did all the sappy shit that she loved.

A common misconception was that pussy made every man weak. No amount of good pussy could make a strong man weak. I didn't give a fuck if that shit was directly sent from Heaven, pussy didn't make a strong man weak. Pussy made a weak man weaker. It turned that nigga into a fool.

A good woman though, that was the only thing capable of making a strong man vulnerable. The mere idea of losing a good woman would drive any many crazy. I had been there and that was why I never wanted to be in that position again.

"You know what, I'm not even mad about you breaking into the house. I have sushi, the park, and you." Willow got on her tippy toes to kiss my lips. She sat on the plush blanket with her legs underneath her.

She was so damn stunning. The day we first crossed paths played in my head vividly. I wasn't sure how I got as lucky as I did to have a second chance to have her, but I couldn't lose it. No matter what, I had to back out of the deal with Santino, then I would tell her about it.

"How was your day mama?"

Willow stared down at the sushi in front of her, making me uneasy. My body tensed as I awaited her answer. The seconds passed as if they were hours the longer, she took to respond.

"I have to tell you something but I'm afraid to."

"What is it?" A mixture of emotions brewed within me from the unknown.

"It's about Wallace."

My patience began to wear thin with how Willow prolonged what she had to say. Her breathing became sporadic causing me to become anxious. Doing my best to keep her calm, I took a hold of Willow's wrists, drawing her into my lap. Cradling her in my arms, I kissed at her face knowing that would calm her nerves some.

"Wallace? What about Wallace mama? Talk to me please."

Listening to Willow described how Wallace had asked her to fake her death to protect herself from someone he thought would come after him, had my blood boiling.

I was ready to fuck the whole city of Miami up as she continued to tell me Wallace had been dodging her calls until earlier that day. She also clarified that Trinity was very well aware of who Green and I were. She was the one that suggested that Willow come clean to me.

Fear was attached to every word she spoke.

Willow was unsure if she should fake her death like Wallace suggested. It was a wild request but if Willow was in true danger, then I could understand why that would be his go to solution. My main concern was that Willow wasn't about the street life. She was raised in Little Haiti up until the age of eleven, but her mother protected her from that street life.

The only reason she even owned a gun was because I had purchased it for her to teach her how to shoot. She wasn't built for that life and even if she was riding for me, I didn't want her to be a part of that bullshit. Willow was too pure to be around that shit. She was my light in a world of darkness. I was going to do what I had to do to ensure nothing or anyone diminished it.

Not Wallace.

And definitely not Santino.

My mind was going a hundred miles a minute trying to put the pieces of an unsolvable puzzle together. Was the real reason Santino postponed the kill was to get at Wallace by way of Willow? From what I found about him; Wallace was a foul ass lawyer that would do anything for a dollar. Was Santino the only one after him?

I was so damn distracted by getting back in her good graces, I failed to recognize that she was in danger. "Mama, tell me everything you know about Wallace's dealings. Even if it doesn't seem important, tell me it anyway."

While Willow broke down Wallace's life as best as she could, my mind was made up.

Santino had to die, and I was going to be the one to take his life. "I'll take care of it."

"Baby…"

"Mama please don't ask for any details. Have the confidence that I will take care of it. I'll give my life before I allow anything to happen to you."

For Willow to come to me knowing what I was capable of, she knew exactly what my next move would be. No nigga was about to put fear in my woman's heart while I was alive and well. That was what Wallace and his dealings had done. Willow wasn't about to fake her death, but she wasn't going to go around the city without protection either. Santino was after Wallace and that nigga's reach was far. If there were more than one person after Wallace's crooked ass, I had to be prepared for that as well.

"We're still working through this so I'm not going to force myself on you mama. However, there's no way in hell I'm going to have you moving through the city unprotected."

Willow raised her head from my chest. The smile that adorned her face brought a smile to mine. Joy gleamed from her eyes as she teased me. "Is that your way trying to get a key to my house? Are you going to protect me?"

"That weak ass .22 sure as hell isn't going to do it."

"You bought me that gun!" she exclaimed slapping my

chest.

"A year ago. I'm going to have to upgrade you to a Glock .357."

"Grym you know I have no idea what that means."

I went to explain to her the differences between the guns but stopped myself. There was no point in doing so. Until she showed real interest, she wouldn't retain the information. I had only gotten her the .22 because she used to go to the shooting range with me once a week before our separation. Willow wasn't about that life and I never wanted her to be.

"You will. But back to the pressing issue. Whether you give me a key or not, we both know I can get in."

She giggled and laid her head back on my chest. "Yeah you've proven that twice already. Thank you."

"What you thanking me for mama?"

"For loving me, protecting me, and being here for me."

"I'll always be here for you mama. I will always love you. And I'll always protect you."

Without verbally giving me permission, Willow gave me the go ahead to handle everything. There was no point in worrying her about the hit that I was ordered to take out on Wallace therefore, I withheld it from her. It wouldn't change anything.

Santino had to die and if Wallace was on some scheming shit, he'd have to go too.

CHAPTER THIRTEEN

Grym

After hanging in the park for a few hours, we decided to head back to the house. Being around Willow had me on cloud nine. Dealing with outside bullshit was taking away from the time that I wanted to spend to her, but I had to do what I had to do. I was never going to neglect my woman nor was I going to let her walk around afraid that something was going to happen.

If Willow was in danger, by extension, Trinity was in danger as well. In the morning, Green and I would have to devise a plan to protect them. It couldn't have come at worst time being that we didn't trust the niggas in his camp. The most loyal one betrayed him; there was no telling who else was on some shady shit. With the high probability that Santino was the one Wallace told Willow about, I really couldn't trust those niggas.

On the way back Willow and I attempted to reach both

Trinity and Green, but neither were answering their phones. Stepping into the house, it was clear why our calls went unanswered.

"Mmhmmm daddy. Yes right there."

Green was hitting Trinity from the back in the middle of the kitchen, butt ass naked. They were so engrossed in the moment; they didn't even notice us standing at the front door.

"You like that shit baby? Tell me how good it feels," Green grunted from the kitchen.

"So fucking good daddy. The dick feels so good."

Willow looked up at me and whispered, "Are they really in the kitchen fucking?"

"That's what it looks like. Again, they're grown. It's none of our business."

Taking her hand, I led her upstairs for our private time. Willow had me wide open. If I was being real with myself, I was more open than before. The need to keep her was stronger than before, because the thought of losing her was always in the back in my mind. In the past, I never thought about it. But having experienced living through it, had a nigga terrified. Death didn't scare me; losing my reason to live again did.

"Get in the shower with me baby." Willow stripped her clothes off in the bedroom before leading us to the bathroom down the hall, as I got undressed.

We stepped into the shower, closing the door behind us. The warm water pecked at our skins as the steam surrounded us. Using my right hand I gently placed it around Willow's neck pushing her against the shower wall. Her chest hiked up and down from the anticipation of what was to come. Lifting her right leg up with my left arm, I pushed my dick into her folds. Her juices dripped down my dick, welcoming me to paradise.

"Mmmhmm," Willow purred.

Each stroke brought a gasp.

Each gasp motivated me to go harder.

The harder I went, the louder she grew.

The louder she grew the more it became impossible to hold my nut in.

"Fuck Willow. I love you mama."

"I love you too baby."

Releasing her neck, I picked up the other leg. With each leg spread as wide as I could get them, I plummeted inside of her until she creamed on my dick, and I planted my seeds inside of her.

After we were done in the shower, we went to back to her bedroom to finish what we started. It was well into three the morning by the time we went to sleep. There was no doubt in my mind that Willow was going to be sore in the morning. She had a nigga trying new positions she couldn't even handle.

Rolling over in bed, I noticed Willow was gone. My eyes shot open in time to see her carrying a tray of food along with two glasses of orange juice while wearing a silk black robe. "I thought we'd have breakfast in bed baby."

That was the thing about Willow. I loved doing the sappy shit she liked because she'd turn around to do the same shit for a nigga. It didn't matter how hard my exterior was, feeling loved by a woman that was technically too good for me, did something to me. I appreciated the essence of her more than anything. Her femininity and gentleness were what made me love her as much as I did.

A woman shouldn't have to be hard all of time. If I got out of pocket, she would boss up on me, and that shit was sexy as hell. As long as it wasn't disrespectful, I was cool with it. I just wasn't with that crazy shit. Some niggas liked women to match their crazy but not me. I already had chaos around me all the time, with my woman, I wanted to be surrounded by peace.

Willow was my calm in the midst of chaos.

She placed the tray on my lap and proceeded to snuggle up under me. I kissed her forehead before taking a bite of my bacon. "What do you want to do today mama?"

Having to handle business would take me away from her, however I always had to set aside time for her. "I want to take you on a date."

"You want to take me on date?" I dropped the bacon on my plate waiting for her to continue.

Willow reached over, grabbed a grape and popped it her mouth. "Yes, I want to take you on a date."

"You sound crazy as hell. Ain't no way I'm letting you take me on a date." Taking a forkful of scrambled eggs, I continued to enjoy my breakfast.

"Why not?"

"Because I'm a man and you're my woman."

"Your woman?"

"Play if you want to Willow. A year apart ain't change

shit. You're mine, and I'm yours." Willow could play all day, but she wasn't going to play with me.

"Okay, I won't take you on a traditional date, but I do have something planned for you."

"You can do that mama." I kissed her on her plump lips as a sign of agreeance.

We made light talk as we finished our breakfast. My phone vibrated accompanied by a text from Green informing me that we had to roll out for the day. I went to reply to his text, but then Willow caught my attention.

"I thought you'd be too sore to get out of bed this morning," I said jokingly.

"You must've forgotten who I was."

Willow winked at me as she laid on her back lifting her legs up to her ears. The sight of her honied nectar seeping from her pretty brown pussy had me forgetting Green and the text he'd just sent me. Stroking my hardened dick, I placed it at her opening. It pulled me in, and I buried myself in between her tight walls. She tightened her grip around my dick causing me to release a groan in the crook of her neck.

Boom Boom Boom

The loud banging on the door went ignored as I went harder trying to catch my nut.

"Grym, nigga you better not be in there fucking. Nigga finally get some pussy after a year and now he can't reply to damn texts." His voice faded as his feet carried him away from the door.

"Shit, that's it baby. Cum in me baby."

Willow didn't have to tell me that. My pull-out game was weak as fuck. With a pussy like Willow's that shit was nonexistence.

"Cum with me mama," I commanded.

My breathing became sporadic as Willow dropped her legs, her body began shuddering, succumbing to her climax. And I was right behind her.

I rolled on to my side of bed trying my best not to fall into a coma. Good pussy made a nigga doze off. But incredible magic pussy, that had a nigga slipping in and out of a coma with no mercy. Once I was sure that my knees wouldn't give out on me, I got up, freshened up, and got dressed. "Share your location with me so I can make sure you're safe until I get back mama."

"Okay baby."

After promising Willow that I would call her after handling business, I headed to meet Green who was outside waiting by the car.

"About time nigga."

"Shut your ass up. I ain't say shit when we walked in on you blowing Trinity's back out in the kitchen," I quipped.

The grin that came across his face was followed by a loud laughter. "Oh shit. You saw that?"

Refusing to engage in his antics, I got in my car. There was a lot he and I had to discuss, and I wasn't sure exactly where to start. "You heard from Santino?"

"Nah, why?"

I went into detail about what Willow told me about Wallace's warning. That someone may go through her trying to get at him. I told him I chose not to tell Willow about the hit I was supposed to carry out on Wallace. That was the last thing that she needed to hear. What really mattered was that it wouldn't be me that carried out the hit.

"To be real with you man, Trinity told me that same shit last night. That nigga is a clown for asking Willow to fake her death. Then the fuck nigga wasn't even answering her calls."

Taking my eyes off the road momentarily, I glanced over at Green. "Nigga y'all pillow talking already?"

"Fuck you Grym!" he belted.

"Did you tell her that I was supposed to take a hit out on Wallace?"

"Nigga you know me better than that. I ain't mentioned that to T. She knows who we are subsequently she wanted to make sure her cousin was protected. I'm going to marry the girl but she ain't my wife yet for me to be telling her everything."

"Subsequently? G I ain't ever heard you use that word. Trinity got you gone like that nigga? On top of that, this nigga talking about getting married."

"You ain't shit. You know that?"

"Never claimed to be."

I looked over in time to catch Grym shaking his head at me. "And you never will be. What you thinking?"

"Man honestly, I was wanting to put some of your boys on them but after Marco, I don't trust that shit at all. I already know at least one nigga is getting laid out when we make it to the warehouse. Then she hinted at giving me a key, which isn't going to work. It's too easy for me to break into their house. The only option is to have them with us in Miami. That way, we can keep them close and protected."

"I was thinking the same thing. There's only one problem to that plan."

"What's that?"

"I don't mind Trinity staying at my place but what if some random stop by?"

"What you mean?"

"Man she had me text every female in my phone to let them know that they were getting cut off before she let me eat her pussy."

"So you done hoeing."

"I told you I was going to be done when I found my wife didn't I?"

Green sounded serious. If Trinity, was anything like Willow, that nigga was going to be buying flowers and shit, every other day. I couldn't even recall a time that nigga bought a female any type of gift. The rest of the way to the warehouse we brainstormed over what was going to take place. We had to cut the heads of the snakes crippling Green's business.

When we made it there, I said, "Let's get this shit done. After that my focus is on Santino. If he's a threat to Willow's life, I have to take him out."

That was Green's connect because he had the best product coming out of Columbia, but any threat to Willow's life was a guaranteed death penalty.

"Say less nigga." We nodded in agreeance before getting out of the car.

I went into my trunk to pull out some of my favorite toys. It was early as hell, but death came when it came, and I was the delivery man. Green always took the lead when handling his team. But I was around just to re-inforce; a betrayal to Green was a betrayal to me. And that was punishable by death.

Inside, there were twenty-three niggas we considered family lined up in the middle of an empty warehouse. Some wore blank expressions while others wore ones of fear. They all soon turned to fear when I dropped the black duffel bag at my feet.

"I don't have all day so we're going to have to make this shit simple as hell. Big Wayne and Honcho step out of line for me," G commanded.

Both men took a step forward. The horror etched on their faces didn't move me in the least. They worked hand in hand with Marco. Green continued, "Do you have anything to say for yourselves?"

Big Wayne was the biggest nigga on the team yet as soon as his mouth opened, he was the biggest bitch. "Boss, I wanted to tell you how Marco was moving but he threat-ened to kill my baby mama."

His excuse was just that—an excuse. Green had way more pull than Marco. If he truly feared for his baby mama's life he would've went straight to Green. For him not to have said anything meant that fat fuck was getting a cut. Sweat dripped down his face as his beady black eyes shifted from left to right.

Honcho spoke up next. "On some real shit, I suspected

that shit but didn't have no proof to bring to you. Marco was closer to you then I was, there was no way I could bring any info to you when I didn't have any real intel."

He kept eye contact with Green the entire time. There was validity in his statement. Other than each other, Green and I didn't fully trust no nigga but if there was a nigga that was close, Marco was the one. Honcho was next in the line for Green and so far, he had been doing good to prove himself.

Bending down, I unzipped my bag to remove a nicely sharpened machete. Without warning I took two clean swipes at Big Wayne's fat ass neck. His head fell on the ground and rolled to my feet as his body went crashing down. Five niggas with weak stomachs threw up at the sight of blood and his lifeless decapitated body sprawled out on the concrete floor.

My part was done.

I left Green to handle the rest of the meeting while I waited for him by the car. Pulling my phone out, I checked Willow's location to see if she was at home. After confirming she was safely at home, I stuffed my phone back in my pocket.

Green's problem had been solved for the most part. Now all of my focus would be geared towards Wallace and Santino.

The Grym Reaper was only getting started.

CHAPTER FOURTEEN

Willow

"What happened to 'Green is a friendly ass nigga with community dick. Ain't no nigga of mine about to have me out here looking crazy because he lacks self-control'?" I used air quotes to emphasize her words.

It was obvious she was playing hard to get. It was even more obvious when I walked in on her holding on to her ankles while Green did his thing. The two were like fire and gasoline it could go super well or it could go super bad. Ultimately, it would be up to them to decide.

"Him being a friendly nigga with community dick hasn't changed. That nigga is still that." Trinity shrugged her shoulders while eating the breakfast I had prepared.

"How did it happen?"

She rolled her eyes. "After he threw my plate away, I went off on him. How childish can he be?"

"That still doesn't explain how he had you bent over calling him daddy." I folded my arms across my chest.

Trinity could play slow all she wanted but if she wasn't going to be honest with me, she had to at least be honest with herself. There was more to her and Green than she was letting on. Trinity was a serial dater however, she was stingy as hell with her pussy.

Standing up, Trinity carried her plate over to the kitchen sink. She then returned to her seat at our small dining room table. She was battling with telling me the truth. If she were to tell me the truth, she couldn't deny what was to become of them.

"Okay fine. I like him. His light bright ass is fine as fuck. And those green eyes have my pussy wet every time I look into them. He's funny and rugged. That's the shit I like."

"Then what's the issue?" I asked concerningly

Her shoulders fell as sadness appeared in her light brown eyes. "Niggas like Green don't change, Willow. That nigga is a kingpin. He got pussy coming at him from every which direction. Not to mention, I left that street life back in Little Haiti. That life isn't the life I want anymore."

"Did you tell him that because in my opinion, he wants more than a situationship with you."

"We talked about it last night…"

"Before he had you bent over or after?" I smirked at Trinity as she narrowed her eyes on me.

"Why can't you let that shit go?"

"Because y'all asses was ass naked in the kitchen, Trinity. He had you calling him daddy and everything sis." Unable to control myself, I laughed hysterically. I wasn't even mad they fucked in the kitchen. It was funny that she wanted to act like he didn't have her calling him daddy, after she called his dick little.

Embarrassment took over her. "You heard that?"

"The whole neighborhood heard it."

She joined in my laughter. "Damn. All I'm saying is that Green proved me to be a liar and I'm leaving it at that."

Throwing my hands in surrender, I replied, "That's fine with me."

"But in all honesty, I'm not built for the life he's living anymore. I want safety. A nigga that gets up in the morning to go to the office and returns to me safely each night. Him and Grym left out this morning, ain't no telling what they are out doing."

"A nigga that goes to office in the morning is the one that put me in danger," I stated referring to Wallace.

Trinity remained silent, permitting me to continue, "T, if nobody understands what you're going through, know that I do. I left Grym after finding out he was an assassin. A year later, I'm back with him with no plans on ever letting him go. It takes acceptance. You pointed that out to me. Do you think you could accept Green?"

"Yes and that shit is terrifying. I thought being rude to him would keep him away, but it did the complete opposite. He cut off all the women in his contacts when I joked with him that it would be the only way that I'd let him taste my pussy. His lifestyle scares me because I used to live it."

"I can't make your decision for you cousin. All I want is for you to be happy. Grym and I had that conversation already. If you want the real thing with Green, you'll have to do the same."

Instead of addressing what I had said, Trinity changed the subject to ask if I had spoken to Grym about the Wallace situation. "What did Grym say?"

"He said he'd take care of it. I didn't ask how because well, you know…"

"Yeah I do."

All of me hated having to put Grym in that position. Yet a part me of me knew it was the best thing for me to do. He had me sharing my location with him to ensure that he knew my whereabouts until he could come up with a plan to find out who was after my stepfather.

For the rest of the day, I stayed at home cleaning up and going over the files of my clients. Grym checked in often enough to where I wasn't missing him too much. Trinity spent most of her time in the living room writing poem after poem. Whenever she wanted to process her feelings, she sat in the living room for hours with a glass of red wine, her notebook, and a pen.

My phone buzzed with an incoming call. When I saw it was Wallace calling, I answered, "Hey Wallace."

"Willow, sweetie, have you made a decision as to what you're going to do? Time is running out and I promised your mom I'd always make sure that you were safe."

"What do you mean time is running out? What time?" My breathing became erratic as my anxiety began to get the worst of me. My bedroom walls began to close in on me the more my mind scrambled to make sense of what Wallace was saying.

"I can't talk right now sweetie. I'll call you at the end of the week for a final decision. To keep you out of harm's way, we must act fast. We both know that I am not your biological father nevertheless, you're my daughter sweetie. You're the only person I have in this world."

As I went to respond, Wallace hung up cutting me off. With a dozen different thoughts running through my head, I dropped my phone on my bed and took off downstairs to find Trinity still on the couch.

"Willow, what's wrong? You're shaking."

My legs were barely keeping me up as I replayed Wallace's last words to me. "Trinity what am I going to do?"

"Do about what? Talk to me, Willow."

"I just got off the phone with Wallace. He told me I had until the end of the week to give him an answer on what I was going to do."

"The end of the week? You need to call Grym. I'll cancel my date with Quan to stay here with you until he gets back," Trinity comforted me.

"Cancel your date? Nah, you're about to cancel the whole nigga," Green's voiced boomed from the front door. I wasn't sure when they showed up. It was more than likely Grym took my house key again.

"Green this ain't the time," Trinity seethed.

"No it's the perfect time. Grym got his lady. Call that nigga and cancel him now, T." The two of them stared at each other intensely daring the other to back down. When I saw Trinity dial a number and put the phone up to her ear, I knew that Green had won.

Grym walked over, picked me up, and carried me up the stairs. When we were alone in my room, I ran down the conversation between myself and Wallace. "Baby, maybe I should fake my death. It would make everything easier, and keep me protected."

"Mama, it's not as easy as you think to fake your death. Wallace is acting as if it is, but I can tell you it's not. I'll keep you protected. Pack whatever you'll need to stay with me while I put my plan together."

"What about Trinity?"

"She's going to stay with Green."

My eyes widened at that news. "Umm, that's not a good idea.'"

"They are grown mama. I can promise you, Green isn't going to hurt her. She'll probably hurt that nigga first," he joked.

"Yeah you're right." I giggled envisioning Green's reaction when he found out that Trinity had a date the day after they were together. He was big mad.

"Pack your bags while I go to talk to Green, mama. I love you."

"I love you too baby."

There was comfort in knowing that Grym would do anything to protect me. Our love was meant to ride for. For the first time in a long time, I felt complete safety in being worry free.

And it all had to with Grym.

CHAPTER FIFTEEN

Grym

For the past couple of days things had been stagnant. There was no new information coming in if there was someone else after Wallace. Santino was the only nigga that was out for that nigga's head and even he had been quiet for far too long.

Wallace wasn't having meetings outside of his normal ones. The database system at his law office was easy as hell to hack, so I had his weekly schedules from day one. Other than the one-time Willow visited him, Wallace didn't have any at home visitors.

The only thing that was keeping me sane was Willow being in Miami with me. I didn't have to worry about her being too far away if something was to happen. My house was more secure than hers. She and Trinity took a week off to allow Green and I time to put a plan together. That was the part that proved to be the hardest.

Taking Santino out wasn't going to be easy, but it wasn't impossible either. The only problem was, we were unsure he was the only one that had it out for Wallace.

Killing Santino was going to impact Green's business. If we were going to take that risk, we had to be sure Santino was the one that was coming for Wallace, as well as Willow.

Wallace had proved to be on some fraud shit too. He wasn't giving Willow any information on what was going on with him. That shit was pissing me off and had me ready to knock him off. After conversing with Green, I decided to not kill him for Willow's sake. But I was slowly beginning to reconsider not killing him when everything was said and done.

"We have to come up with a plan. The week is coming to a close," Green said. We were sitting out in his backyard while I gave Willow time to focus on her work without any interruptions. Every hour of the day my head was buried in her pussy or ass. If it wasn't that, I was knee deep inside of her.

"Santino is the only one we know of."

"Then do what you have to do. That nigga is fucking with family if he's coming for Willow. Him calling off the hit temporarily got me looking at that nigga sideways."

Green confirmed what I was feeling. "Yeah that's the same thing I was thinking. He was determined for me to end Wallace. I missed the first opportunity, that was all me. Yet, whenever I went to complete the job, he called it off. Like the nigga went to plan B or some shit."

"Santino is a grimy nigga. My right mind is telling me that it's him."

"Yeah mine too."

"Then that nigga is as good as dead."

"The Grym Reaper is coming for him. Give me two days to orchestrate everything. You'll go out of town with Trinity and Willow. I'll come after I complete the job."

Green blew out the smoke from his blunt. "Nah, you not going to do this alone."

"Green, he's your connect. You can't be anywhere near that shit. If there is any suspicion about you then how are you going to get another one nigga?" I understood that his loyalty lied with me but Green needed to not think with his emotions.

"That shit don't matter nigga. I'm thinking about retiring soon anyway."

We had settled on retiring at t thirty-five. We were three years from that. "Retire?"

"Yeah bro. Trinity is crazy as fuck but in the short time she's been staying me she's proven to be solid. She has her own business, she's smart ass fuck. Grym, the girl will sit up on my couch and write a poem that will have me reevaluating my entire life nigga. We cook together, we laugh together, and she ain't checking for what I can do for her even though I'm prepared to do everything. Trinity's focus is on how we can grow together. She's always on some deep philosophical shit."

"Trinity? The same Trinity that said you couldn't make a virgin call you daddy?" The two had gotten close but no one could've predicted that outcome from either one of them.

"Man I'm still punishing her ass for saying that weak shit." He took a puff of his blunt before continuing, "She made it clear to me that she accepts me. But on some real shit bro, she doesn't want that street life. As for me,

I'm tired of watching you cut niggas' heads off with machetes. I'm holding off until everything dies down with Santino, and then pulling out. You should do the same bro."

"Yeah you're right." It was time for both of us to retire. We had enough money and businesses set up to live well above our means. Willow wasn't going to put pressure on me to do so. As a man that had vowed to love and protect her, I made the choice that was best for our future.

"You trying to trap her ain't you nigga?" Green asked with the blunt in between his lips. The smirk on his face had me smiling hard ass fuck.

"Nah I'm trying to start a family nigga," I corrected him.

Now more than ever, I wanted to create the nuclear family I never had. My children would have a loving father and mother that raised them right. No way in hell did I want my son to be in the lifestyle I chose. They were going to be born into generational wealth not around drugs, guns, and murder. Green and I lived the life we did out of necessity. Wasn't shit glamorous about the long nights, the losses, and risking our freedom. Once we were gone our names would die down in the streets like many before us. The only ones that could carry our names were our wives and future children. We had to do right by them while we could.

"Me too but I'm trying to trap her too. It's only been a week and I swear I damn near called up the jeweler to get her an engagement ring this morning."

Hearing Green continuously talk about marriage was wild as fuck to me. Two weeks ago, the nigga had a girl he was fucking off with tied up in the trunk of her own damn car. Yet there he was, talking about making Trinity his wife and mother to his future children.

"That's some real shit. I'm about to head out and get back to my lady."

Trinity and Willow had plans to have dinner tomorrow at Green's house. Going out wasn't an option for them. The goal was to keep Willow out of the public since we didn't know what Santino knew about her. We were walking around blind, therefore we had to be extremely cautious.

After I left Green's home, I stopped by the floral shop to get a bouquet of flowers for Willow. Having her in my home was like traveling down memory lane. She and I practically lived together before our separation. Every night when I went home, I'd bring her a dozen red and white roses. Since she was back staying with me, I decided to start our routine back up.

Opening the front door I was greeted with the smell of home cooked food, vanilla scented candles, and Willow in a black lace teddy.

"What did I do to deserve this?"

"Be the best husband a woman could ask for."

My eyes watered at Willow the sight of Willow wearing her wedding band. It was her first time calling me her husband in over a year. She and I had gotten married three months into our relationship. When we had our first date, there was no doubt in my mind that she was the woman that housed my rib. We didn't see a point in waiting when fate had brought us together. I was more than grateful that she was ready to wear that title proudly again.

Willow was my serenity in the midst of chaos.

The leaves on the branches of a willow tree symbolized nature, fertility, and life. It also represented balance, learning, growth, and harmony. The willow tree itself represented strength and stability. The structure of the trunk stood firm, withstanding the greatest of challenges.

Willow represented all of those things in my life. I wasn't whole before her, and I wasn't whole when she left me. Seeing her stand in front of me looking sexy as fuck in all of her chocolate glory had my dick on hard.

She glided over to me. "We have steak, potatoes, and grilled asparagus. Since I couldn't take you on a date, I decided to bring dinner to you."

"Fuck dinner. I want dessert mama."

"And you'll get that all night long. You have to eat first baby."

Willow took the flowers from me, turned around, and strolled into the kitchen. My eyes stayed focused on her bouncing ass. I was apprecíative of the dinner she cooked for a nigga, but her ass was the only thing I hungered for at the moment. She returned with a plate of food in one hand and a glass of brown liquor in the other.

"Come have a seat baby."

Sauntering over to my black leather couch, I sat down. The smell of the food caused my stomach to growl. She handed me my plate and I went right into the steak. That shit was so juicy it had me envisioning how juicy her pussy would be on my lips. I was so engulfed in my food I didn't notice Willow get down on her knees.

I held my breath as she unbuckled my belt and released my dick that was up and ready. Willow swallowed me whole. Her spit ran down my dick causing me to release a moan. The way her lips moved up and down my dick had me in trance. When I couldn't take it anymore, I sat my food to the side, picked her up, and bent her over the couch. Picking up the glass from the coffee table, I poured it down her ass for me to lick up every drop.

Willow hissed as I went down to her pretty pussy that was teasing me. Inserting my tongue inside of her tight hole, I began to maneuver it in out. Her juices coated my tongue and I knew she was ready to have me.

Standing up, I entered her as her tight walls hugged my dick. "Fuck mama. I fucking love you!"

"I love you too baby," she said through her heavy breathing.

"Say you'll never leave me. Say that shit."

"I'll never le… lea… leave youuuuuu," Willow sung. "I'm about to cum baby. Shit Grym! I'm about to cum!"

Giving her two more strokes hitting her spot, Willow unhinged as she squirted all over my dick. Her body shook as I got down to drink as much of her juices as I could. Once I was done, I slapped her on the ass. "I love you wife."

"I love you too husband."

Willow Jones.

My wife.

She was riding for me.

She was riding for love.

CHAPTER SIXTEEN

Willow Jones

"Trinity, me putting that ring back on had Grym turning into a whole other beast last night."

She and I were having sushi at Green's house. With me living with Grym, and her living with Green, we didn't have much time to ourselves.

"What you mean?"

"He poured D'ussé down my ass and then licked it up!"

Trinity fell from the couch dramatically. "Y'all not about to outdo me and Green. I'm going to have that nigga eat edibles from my ass crack."

Unable to contain myself, I belted out laughing. "That nigga would happily do that shit too."

"You ain't ever lied. If he could smoke a blunt from my ass crack, he would."

"Something is seriously wrong with the two of you."

"Nah, everything is right with us. Green gets all the sides

of me. He loves hippy me, hood me, crazy me, loving me, and freaky me."

"So y'all really doing this?"

It was refreshing to see Trinity committed to someone. For as long as I could remember, she only allowed people to see certain parts of her because she was afraid no man would accept all of her. She was a complex person with multiple layers. Only someone deserving should have gotten that privilege—Green was that person.

"Yeah, he finessed the fuck out of me."

"What about Quan?" I hated to ask, but I felt like I had to.

"That green eyed muthafucka made me call Quan to cut him off last week at the house." She rolled her eyes while getting back on the couch. "I'm not mad about it though."

"So does that mean you're good here?"

"Yes, I'm happy. Green is super sweet when he's not being an asshole." If my cousin was happy then I was happy. "But ummm, let's talk about the shit you and Grym been hiding. I still can't believe y'all asses are married. That's why you had a damn P.O. Box instead of using the address to get mail. To think I ain't ever seen your damn IDs laying around."

When Grym and I got married, I chose to keep our marriage a secret because I didn't want to hear what people had to say. I didn't want to hear any negativity about us not waiting long enough to get married. Love came when it came, and nobody could do shit to stop it.

Trinity and I continued to make small talk until my phone rang. Wallace's name popped up causing my heart to sink. He was supposed to call me at the end of the week. I was hoping that Grym would've had everything taken care of prior to me receiving the call.

"Hello."

"Willow, sweetie, time has run out sooner than I thought it would. What are you going to do?"

Wallace was still keeping me in the dark as to who and what had him on the time clock that determined my faith. The last time he and I spoke, he told me that he planned on getting out of town. "I'm not going to do it. I can't leave everything behind."

"Willow I promised your mother I would always take care of you," he attempted to reason with me. "This is the only way I know how sweetie."

I had Grym to take care of me.

To protect me.

To devote himself to me.

To love me.

"You don't have to carry that burden anymore." I hung up the phone right as he went to protest.

Trinity stared at me with curiosity in her eyes. "What did Wallace say?"

"That time has run out."

"What the fuck does that even mean? If this nigga knows who is coming for him why the fuck won't he tell you?"

"Honestly, I don't know. It's like he knows someone is coming for him and he's afraid they might come for me too. We need to get to the house and tell the guys."

Trinity and I rushed around the house gathering together our belongings, trying to get to Grym's house as fast as we could. It was the house that I had called home for four months of our marriage. Marrying Grym was the best decision I had ever made. There was one thing I was certain about in life and it was that light skin muthafucka was meant to be my husband. The more time I spent in the house, the more I adjusted to my role as his wife.

As I entered the house, I heard Grym and Green engaged in an intense conversation from Grym's office. "Tomorrow I'm taking out Santino. You're taking the girls out of town. There's something I don't trust about Wallace. The way that nigga is handling Willow isn't sitting well with me. I should've taken that nigga out when I had the chance."

"If you would've killed him weeks ago, we wouldn't be here now. There's good and bad in that. Everything happens for a reason bro," Green stated

"You're right. Santino wanting me to take out Wallace was like a damn domino effect."

My mouth dropped at the revelation that Grym was the one after my stepfather. The entire time I was confiding in him, he knew everything. I backed away, knocking over a vase of red and white roses. As I tried to scramble back to the living room, I heard Grym and Green's footsteps.

"Trinity, we have to go now."

Trinity was on the couch eating a small bowl of grapes. "Where we going? Did you tell Grym what Wallace said?"

"What did Wallace say?" Grym's voice came blasting from behind me.

I turned around to face the man I trusted with my life. There was no way I could run away, not the way I did last time. We were going to force a way to talk it through. "I heard you and Green."

His eyebrows furrowed but he didn't break eye contact with me. "What did you hear?"

"You are the one. You're the one that's after Wallace. You're the one after me."

Grym pinched the brim of his nose as a sign that he was frustrated. "Mama you have to let me explain."

"Were you hired to kill Wallace before we reconnected?"

"Yes but…"

I cut him off. "Was Wallace how you found me?"

"Yes but…"

"I told myself that I wouldn't walk away from you the way I did a year ago. I gave you a chance to express yourself but know that we are done for good."

Green and Trinity stood by silently observing our exchange. They would have to picks sides; we all were well aware of where their allegiance lied.

The second Grym took a step towards me I threw my purse at his head, but he dodged it, pissing me off even more. I was sick of being calm.

Sick of being passive.

I was sick and tired.

I was fucking tired of him not fully opening up to me. I'd been accepting him for who he was and what he did, without any judgement. How dare he trick me into trusting him again, when he didn't even trust me.

"Don't you come near me, you light skin muthafucka. We are done. Trinity let's go."

Rushing out the front door, he didn't bother to try to stop me. No good would've come from it. I fumed as I waited in the car for Trinity to come out to join me. As soon as she got in the car she tried to reason with me, "Grym would never do anything to hurt you."

"But he keeps secrets from me."

"For your own good though."

Ignoring her I peeled out of the drive way to head back to Fort Lauderdale. There was no way in hell I was going to go to Green's. Grym was probably going to head straight there once he thought I cooled down some.

"Where are you going?"

"We are going back to Fort Lauderdale. We aren't in no fucking real danger. Grym was hired to kill Wallace. Instead, he's going to kill San somebody. I'm not dealing with this."

"Willow you're not thinking straight. Let's go to Green's."

My anger got the best of me hearing Trinity plead Grym's case. "Hell no! Fuck him!"

The ringing of my phone through the speakers interrupted our heated conversation right as I went to get on the interstate. Just my luck—it was Wallace.

"Wallace I can't talk right now."

"Trinity this is important. Go to my bank. I'll meet you there for to give you some money to get the hell out of Miami."

The worry in his voice had my nerves rattling as I made

a U-Turn in the middle of the street. Trinity was sitting up in her seat as I raced down the street. Luckily, the they were bare and there were no cops in sight.

"What the fuck Willow?"

"Trinity call Green and tell him what's going on?"

Green answered Trinity's call on the first ring. "Babe, y'all good?"

"Where's Grym?" I yelled since she had the call on speaker phone.

"He's here. What's going on?" Green's voice got deeper with panic.

"Wallace called for Willow to meet with him at the bank. Something is up. Can you meet us there?"

"Which bank?" Green quizzed

"Chase on Second Ave," I yelled out.

Grym's voice was muffled in the background and then I heard it clear as day. "Willow turn the fucking car around now! Do not go to that damn bank! Get back here."

No sooner than his words registered, three black SUV's surrounded me, forcing me to hit the brakes. Our bodies jerked as the car came to a stop. A man in a ski mask came to my door and busted out my driver's side window. Trinity and I screamed praying that Grym and Green would, miraculously teleport to save us.

"What the fuck is going on?" I heard Grym yell over mine and Trinity's screams. Another man came to the passenger side. We fought as hard as we could but the harder, we fought, the more force the men used. Out the corner of my eyes I was able to see a license plate.

"GVQZ34. Florida tag!" I screamed at the top of my lungs praying that one of them heard me through all of the commotion.

The man pulling me from the car, lifted his gun, slamming the butt of it on my head.

Everything went black.

CHAPTER SEVENTEEN

Grym

While Willow was out the house, I elaborated my plans of taking Santino out, with Green in my home office. Everything was in place to handle him. For Willow's sake, I had decided to not complete the job on Wallace, though I was beginning to reconsider.

"Tomorrow, I'm taking out Santino. You're taking the girls out of town. There's something I don't trust about Wallace. The way that nigga handling Willow is suspect. I should've taken that nigga out when I had the chance."

"His poor decisions put Willow in fucked up position, but you have to see all sides of this. If you would've killed him weeks ago, we wouldn't be here now. There's good and bad in that. Everything happens for a reason bro," Green applied some logic.

"You're right. Santino wanting me to take out Wallace was like a damn domino effect."

The shattering of glass disrupted our conversation. Breaking into my house was impossible, so I knew for certain it was Willow. Rushing out the office I found her in the living room convincing Trinity they needed to leave.

I never intended for her to find out about my contract on Wallace, let alone the way she'd found out. If Willow would've given me a real opportunity to explain things to her, she'd understand why I withheld that information from her. The way Willow's mind worked she probably thought I knew her life was in danger before her telling me about Wallace. In the state she was in there would be no convincing her otherwise.

She walked out on me and I allowed her to. No matter what Willow said, she and I weren't done. The space she required would be given to her. However, once she calmed down, I'd be right in her face helping her getting her mind right.

"You good?" Green asked me.

I finished pouring my drink. "Nigga do I look good? My heart just walked out on me for a second time. How the fuck am I losing control of this situation?"

"There's no amount of planning you can do that can prepare you to deal with a woman's emotions bro. Trinity's crazy ass taught me that."

Taking a gulp, I refilled my glass back up. "Nigga it ain't even that. I don't even care that she knows I was hired to kill Wallace because I was going to back out of that shit for her. What I care about is her thinking that I might've used her for that reason."

"Why would she think that?"

"When we originally met, I had no idea she was a software engineer. As we got more acquainted she told me about her profession. She taught me a lot of the shit that I know about hacking. After finding out what I did, she left because she thought I used her to better my skills."

"But you didn't."

"Nigga ain't that what I just said?" Pinching the brim of my nose, I began pacing my living room.

Willow and Trinity were out of protection which was another problem. Green had gotten Trinity to share her location with him so that we would be able to keep tabs on them. Until I saw Santino take his last breath, I wouldn't be able to sleep.

"Trinity's calling," Green announced. "Babe, y'all good?"

"Where's Grym?" Willow yelled out

"He's here. What's going on?" Green's voice deepened as where my words caught in my throat. My gut was telling me something had gone wrong

"Wallace called for Willow to meet him at the bank. Something is up. Can you meet us there?" Trinity clarified.

"Which bank?" Green quizzed

"Chase on Second Ave," Trinity yelled out.

Something was definitely going on. Wallace had left her out to fend for herself and then all of a sudden, he was asking her to meet with him at the bank. "Willow turn the fucking car around now! Do not go to that damn bank! Get back here."

The sound of tires screeching, glass breaking, and my

woman screaming, had me seeing red. "What the fuck is going on?"

Trinity and Willow's screamed burned my ears as Green and I ran to the back of my house to my gun room. I was fucking pissed. If Willow hadn't overheard me than she wouldn't be in danger. My breathing became labored as I tried my best to keep my composure. I wasn't sure where to start but if I had to burn down the whole city to find them, I had no issues doing so.

"GVQZ34. Florida tag!" Willow yelled right as the call ended.

"GVQZ34! Text that to me," I commanded Green.

I silently thanked the Almighty for Willow's quick thinking. She gave me the first clue to finding out who had taken her. There was no doubt it was Santino's people, but the situation had become complex. The clean kill that I had planned was out the window. Everyone attached to that nigga was about to feel my wrath.

Grabbing two duffel bags, I filled them with as many weapons as I could. Green was silent which was a good sign. Whenever he got that way, it meant that nigga was ready for war. Handing him one of the duffle bags, we left the house, headed to my van in the garage.

Once we were in, I pulled out my laptop and looked up who the tag was registered to. One thing was for sure, whoever Santino hired, they were some fucking amateurs. That would only make my job of getting to them easier.

The picture of who the car was registered to popped up and Green finally broke his silence. "That's Marco's people."

"What?"

"Yeah, that's his older brother, Lonzo. That nigga was never good at this shit, so I put him out, allowing Marco to step up. He got in the game soon as you got out but didn't last long."

The more I distanced myself from the drug game, the less I cared to know about the people involved. The people I knew were cool, and I was never one to make new friends. As long as Green was good, shit else didn't matter to me. Lonzo wasn't even at the cookout when we were,

"What the fuck is really going on?" I squeezed my steering wheel as my anger intensified.

"This is somehow tied to Santino. You got an address?"

Giving Green the address the car was registered to, I pulled out of my garage. The house was in Liberty City. There wasn't a hood in Miami that we couldn't walk through. When we got to our destination, Green got a call. Retrieving my Beretta M9, silencer, and machete from my duffle bag, I was ready to get whatever information I could pull from anybody. The information we got would determine my weapon of choice.

Green appeared focus as he listened to the person. After hanging up the phone, Green threw it on the floor of the car. "Fuck!"

I was so focused on Willow; I hadn't taken the time to realize how much he was hurting too. Just like Willow had been kidnapped, so had Trinity. "Talk to me G."

"Nigga that was Honcho. After you took out Big Wayne, I assigned him to listen for any information. He just got word that Lonzo kidnapped a lawyer's daughter for Santino. He's hoping that Santino will put him on. That's the shit him and Marco was working on."

The shit was all starting to make sense. If Marco had succeeded at making Green appear like he was shorting Santino, he could persuade Santino to be his connect. Since we had to off Marco, Lonzo had to find another way to get to Santino to earn his trust.

"How we doing this?" Green asked me.

"Have Honcho come up here with the clean-up crew. They have to be careful because it's not all the way dark out yet. We not leaving that house until we get all the info we need. Going to the warehouse doesn't guarantee we're going to find them. Doing it this way, will lure Lonzo to us and we can get to them."

Green nodded as he shot Honcho a text. "Let's do this."

We slipped on our black leather gloves. I secured my Berretta on my waist and carried my machete. Green secured his hip while carrying the other black duffel bag. When we approached the house, I covered the peephole as Green knocked.

A woman's voice came from inside the house. "Who is it?"

"Pizza delivery," I responded. We pulled down our ski masks as we heard her footsteps approaching the door.

The door swung open. "I didn't order any...."

Green pointed the glock in her face with no time to think. She covered her mouth as tears began to trickle down her face. She was a young ass girl; didn't look any older than eighteen. "Where your father at?"

Her body shock as she tried to keep her composure. "My

father?"

"Yeah, Lonzo. Ain't that nigga your father?" I asked. None of my victims had been children, and I hated for her to be the first.

"He's my boyfriend."

"How old are you?" Green and I asked at the same time. Lonzo was older than the both of us. What the fuck was he doing with some young ass girl.

"Seventeen," she stated through her tears.

"You deserve your ass beat for that shit. Fuck is your mama and daddy for you to be sucking that grown nigga's dick?" Green asked.

She remained silent.

Getting agitated, I made her lead us to the kitchen where I tied her up with the rope from the duffle bag that Green brought in. We had her Facetime Lonzo, crying and begging for him to come save her. Her real fear brought life to her performance as she pleaded for him to come by himself. When he saw her, the nigga damn near teared up. Not only was he a bitch, the nigga was a damn pedophile too. Niggas like that deserved to suffer before they died, and I was going to deliver on that.

Honcho texted Green letting him know they were in position and ready for their cue. The orders were simple, take out anyone that even looked like they were affiliated with Lonzo. The young girl may have told him to come alone, but niggas didn't like to listen.

Lonzo came bursting through the door twenty minutes later. Green was hidden while I stood behind the girl with my gun pointed at him and my machete against her neck.

Without Lonzo noticing, Green knocked him out with the butt of his gun.

Honcho and two others from Green's team came in, carrying dead bodies. They were in the car waiting on Lonzo to give them a signal to come in. Honcho took care of them before they could even make it to the front porch.

Getting another chair, Green tied Lonzo up in the living room. Taking out my Beretta with the silencer attached, I shot the girl two times in the dome before going into the living room. Initially, I thought to let her go because she wouldn't be able to identify us but went against that. Even if she couldn't identify us, there was nothing stopping her from going to the police.

When Lonzo regained consciousness, he fought to break free. "Who the fuck are you? What the hell do you want man? I ain't got no money, please let me and my girl go."

I removed my ski mask because I wanted my face to be the last face he saw before he departed the earth. "You a nasty ass muthafucka to be fucking with a child."

"Man is this what this is about? I ain't know she was that young," Lonzo lied.

Green punched that nigga right in his jaw knocking his two front teeth out. Blood spewed from his mouth as he winced from the pain. We were pressed for time therefore I needed for shit to happen fast. I was sick of hearing that nigga's voice.

"Nigga fuck all that shit. The women you kidnapped today, where the fuck did you take them?"

In order to get real information from a person you were

about to kill, you had to ask the right questions. I rarely ever questioned a person's whose life that was dependent of me. People lied when they were desperate. If they could through someone under the bus to save their life, they would. That was why I asked Lonzo a question that couldn't implicate anyone else. He had no choice but to tell me the truth by telling on himself.

"What women?"

This nigga wanted to play stupid, and I didn't like that shit. I ordered Honcho to stuff his mouth with the towel from the bag. I held his arm out and chopped his right hand off with my machete. I didn't have time for any games. "Do you remember what women now?"

He nodded while snot and tears ran down his face. Honcho removed the towel to give him the opportunity to tell me what I wanted to hear. "You don't have to do this man. A Columbian nigga, Santino, had me take them to an abandoned warehouse about thirty minutes out in some huge ass lot. I can give you the exact location. Just please man, I ain't trying to die like this."

Lonzo began sobbing while continuing to beg for his life. After obtaining all the information we needed, I picked up machete and with one swift motion his head came clean off his shoulders. Green and I left out, leaving Honcho and the other two men to clean up.

"Why can't you just shoot a nigga?"

"Niggas see niggas getting shot every day G. A machete really be putting fear in these niggas."

"You're crazy as hell."

Shrugging my shoulders, I replied. "You ain't seen crazy

yet."

Though I was stressed not knowing how Willow was doing, my spirit was more at ease knowing we were a step closer to getting to her and Trinity. I pulled out into the street to head to the place where it all began.

CHAPTER EIGHTEEN

Willow

When I came to, Trinity and I were tied up in a small rusty metal room. My eyes flashed around the room, searching for exits. The room was windowless and the metal door had no handle, only a small slit between the bottom and where it met the floor. The cold concrete shocked my skin like penetrating bullets. The recent events flooded my mind like flashes of light. I couldn't let my fear outweigh my will for us to make it out. My hands were tied behind my back and my feet were tied together. There was an excruciating pain shooting from the back of my head.

"Trinity, wake up." I scooted closer to her. Her chin was tucked into her chest while her back rested against the wall.

"Shut up bitch, I'm trying to play dead."

"Dead from what Trinity?"

"Blunt force trauma to the head."

We were in the worst predicament possible, and she wasn't making jokes but how was I supposed to take that seriously? Grym and Green were probably searching for us, but we had to boss the fuck up too.

"We need a plan," I nodded to my tied feet.

"What can we do? Those niggas took everything, even our shoes."

We were clothed in only our bras and panties. "Let's try to untie each other and when they get back, we fight them."

"First things first, we don't know how many of them there are. Two, they got guns, Willow. Three, this isn't a movie or a book. We are in a real fucked up situation," Trinity broke down.

"I know that. But we can't sit here, waiting to die either."

"Do you think they'll find us?"

I didn't want to think about that, I was trying my best not to. The facts stared at me in the face. Grym was hired to kill Wallace. He knew that Wallace was my step-father before I confided in him. The fact of the matter was, who-ever kidnapped us could've been the person who hired Grym, and I was just a means to an end.

I was silently battling between logic and my heart.

Logic undoubtedly pointed at Grym's involvement.

My heart reassured me Grym wouldn't deliberately hurt me.

"They're trying to, I know it. I hope they got the plate number I yelled out." Trinity nodded as we sat there in the cold, dark, metal box. My mind raced, searching my thoughts for what we could use to untie each other. The room was bare from what I could see.

The heavy metal door slid open revealing a short Latino man, that looked to be in his fifties at least. He ordered two of his men to lift me and Trinity and had us carried to the main part of the warehouse. They removed the bonds from our feet but kept our hands tied. Once we were seated facing him, he sent one outside to keep guard. My anxiety was through the roof as the reality set in that we were possibly facing the last moments of our lives.

I was too frightened to cry.

I was too terrified to beg for my life.

I was too afraid.

"Ms. Willow do you know why you're here?" The older man spoke to me.

"No," I lied.

"Well senorita, it's because your father doesn't know how to keep good on his promise."

Trinity and I shot each other a look. We were aware that Wallace was the cause, but we were curious as to how.

"You on the hand senorita," he pointed at Trinity, "were simply in the wrong place at the wrong time."

My head spun as I realized Trinity was only here because of me. I should've had left Grym's house alone instead of convincing her to come with me. I mouthed out 'I'm sorry' to her praying that she would forgive me. She shook her head at me and for the first time since the whole ordeal started, I teared up. It was one thing for me to be involved but to have her there made me feel worse.

The older man offered us a sinister smile as he beckoned, "Wallace."

Wallace came into the light without as much as a scratch on his pale thin skin. Surely if they had manhandled him like they did our asses, he wouldn't been red and purple.

"Tell her Wallace," he ordered

"Tell me what?"

Wallace was sweating profusely, doing his best to avoid eye contact with me. My anger rose as the notion of Wallace having more of a hand in the situation than he'd let on.

"For once in your pitiful life, have some balls. You accepted a job to defend my nephew. My namesake, my heir, the one that was to grow my empire when I'm gone, and you failed. The only payment I wanted was your life yet you offered me a million dollars."

"Santino, please. Just do it and get it over with," Wallace's weak ass pleaded.

"Nah muthafucka! You tell me!" I yelled.

The longer I stood, hands tied behind my back in only my bra and panties, my fear was replaced with fury. Wallace was on some fraud shit. The man that promised my mom on her death bed that he would take care of me intentionally put me in harm's way. All while claiming the opposite. Staring into his beady eyes, I wished Grym had taken his ass out.

"She's a feisty one." Santino winked at me and the bile rose in my throat. Santino's explanation of Wallace's plan for me to fake my death was all a grand scheme to collect the million-dollar life insurance policy he'd taken out on me. He was going to use the money to pay Santino and keep his life. It was sickening. When I refused to go along with his original plan, Wallace devised another plan to have me kidnapped and killed, which ended up with him still getting the money.

The rage built exponentially as Santino slowly drawled the story out. Though our hands were still very much tied behind our backs, Trinity and I charged towards Wallace. With swift kicks from us both, he toppled to the ground like the weak bitch he was. With every kick I thought of how he called me over under the pretense that he of honoring my dead mother's wishes; a woman that he claimed to have loved and would do anything for.

Every time my bare foot hit him, I thought about the fake sincerity in wanting me to stay protected. His grimy ass really had me looking at Grym sideways for planning to kill him when he deserved far worse than death.

Whatever dealings he had with Santino had nothing to do with me. When my mother passed, Wallace and I barely kept in contact. He sold our family home and moved into a condo in downtown Miami. I didn't see a dime of the insurance money from my mother's passing, he claimed it was used for her funeral. I didn't want to, either. I'd lost the one person I had in the world; that money wasn't going to heal my pain.

When Santino got tired of watching, he ordered the bulky men to stop us. He pushed Trinity and I to the ground, but that didn't stop us from shouting obscenities at Wallace.

"You a whole ass bitch!" Trinity kept yelling.

The level of anger was indescribable. Wallace used me for a payday to save his ass. And when I didn't fall for his trick, he offered my life instead? All I wanted was for my hands to be free so I could whoop his ass. No one should be that shitty. There was no one I wished dead. Wallace changed that. I wanted that nigga dead.

As we fell, Santino's worker went crashing down causing time to stand still as chaos erupted around us. Trinity tugged at me the best way she could for us as we sped crawled to the nearest stack of wooden crates that we could find.

Had we reached our fate? Would my last memory of Grym be walking out on him once again? The second time around was supposed to be better. We were supposed to bask in our love and marriage.

As death steadily approached me, my only regret was not telling him I loved him one more time.

CHAPTER NINETEEN

Grym

Before we pulled up to the warehouse, Green and I had to come up with a strategy that wouldn't end up with the ladies being hurt. We were walking into the situation blind as hell. We weren't certain how many men were inside the warehouse though we had an idea. All we knew for sure was that Santino was in there, and that was where Lonzo had dropped Willow and Trinity.

It was damn near impossible trying to remain calm but successful execution required clear heads. Green was doing surprisingly well. He was quiet. Quiet Green meant deadly Green. According to G, Santino was a cocky muthafucka. He considered himself 'untouchable'.

The nigga thought he didn't need protection. Other than two or three bodyguards, he never had anyone else around. That was to our advantage because the two of us could easily take them out. Although a machete was my weapon of choice for a close kill, I was a beast with my guns. I shot to kill; there was no other way for me.

"We shooting at anything moving."

I looked at Green in the passenger seat sideways. "Nigga you do remember that Willow and Trinity are in there, right? That ain't the way to handle this shit."

"Fuck you want me to do then? Nigga I'm ready to wreck some shit. Fuck the game. Fuck Santino. Fuck all that shit. My fucking heart is in there."

Understanding his agitation, I reasoned with him. "If you weren't my brother, I'd knock the base out your voice. Look G, we can't go in there shooting recklessly. We know for a fact that he's going to have niggas on the outside, we take all out but one."

He listened as I ran the plan down. The one we kept alive, was the key to us getting in. Once inside, we'd assess quickly, then shoot. That was the best approach. Santino kept a small circle of people, so G and I knew there wouldn't be a lot of bodies there. The biggest thing we were avoiding at all costs, either of our women getting caught in the crossfire.

Getting out of the car, I stuffed a Beretta with a silencer in my waist. As tempted as I was to grab my machete, I knew I had to leave it. We had to do the shit as fast as we could to get Willow and Trinity to safety. Once Green secured his gun, we made our way to the warehouse. As expected, there were three men guarding the door. Two of the armed men immediately recognized us from the last visit.

"Mi amigo, what are you doing here tonight?" the shorter, more familiar one asked.

"I'm here to see Santino. Is he in the middle of something?" Green asked.

Without warning, I pulled out one of the guns and let two shots off into the one standing in the middle. Green sent three to the dome of the one the left. Before the last man standing could react, we had our guns drawn out on him.

"I don't want no problems. Whatever you need me to do, I'll do," he pleaded for his life.

"Too late for that shit." I grabbed him and forced him to take the lead heading into the warehouse.

I secured my gun in my waist while Green had his pointed into the guard's back. When he opened the door, my eyes couldn't believe what I was seeing. Wallace was curled up in a ball on the ground beaten. Willow and Trinity were also on the ground with their hands tied behind their backs. It took me all of three seconds to assess the situation. Green let a shot out into the nigga's back where he'd pressed the gun. I sent one flying right between the eyes of the big muthafucka next to Santino. The nigga dropped dead instantly.

From my peripheral vision, I saw Willow and Trinity scrambling to get out the way. Santino tried to retrieve his gun but Green shot him in the right shoulder causing me to drop the gun. The dumbass hadn't even taken off the safety.

"You are finished puto! Finished!" Santino screamed at the top of his lungs.

We offered that nigga no explanation as to why we were there. G ran up on him and landed a right hook to Santino's jaw, causing him to go tumbling down. Blood flowed from his shoulder as he screamed out in agony. I was pretty sure Green knocked his jaw out of place. That shit didn't mean anything. We had all the information we needed. That nigga kidnapped our women, therefore he had to pay the consequences. When he backed out, I assumed that he was on some shady shit. Though, I'd never once thought he was going to go after Willow, to get at Wallace.

While Green handled Santino, I ran in the direction Willow and Trinity ran off in. When I made it around the wooden crates they were hiding behind, they charged at me with their eyes closed.

"Ahhhhhh" Willow screamed while her small fists rained down on me and Trinity kicked at my legs.

"Get y'all little asses off me, it's Grym." I gently pushed them off to restrain them.

They opened their eyes. When Willow's connected with mine, she fell into my chest and cried like she'd been holding tightly to each tear the entire time. Each time I wiped them away, more followed. I quickly untied her and Trinity's bondage.

"Mama it's okay. I'm here. It's all over. I got you. I'll always have you." Picking her up, she wrapped her arms around my neck, and her legs around my waist.

"I love you so much baby. I'm sorry I ever doubted you. Never will I walk away from you again," she managed to say through her sniffles.

"Where's Green?" Trinity asked.

"I'm here baby," Green called out to her. She took off running from behind the crate.

Still carrying Willow who was damn near choking me,

I went to join them. The two were hugging and kissing, like there wasn't three bodies lying a foot in front of them. I finally let Willow down though she kept her tight grip on me. Looking at the lifeless body before me, it was safe to say that Green had taken care of Santino. The blood that covered the concrete floor couldn't be differentiated between his worker, himself, or Wallace.

"We have to get out of here." He took Trinity's hand to lead her out.

As I turned to walk out too, I heard the cocking of a gun, slowly turning, I was looking down the barrel of a gun. Wallace held it firmly in his hand. He hesitated, and that mistake was going to cost him.

When I reached for my gun to grant him the wish he was wishing, I came up empty handed. His finger rested on the trigger and all I could think was, my day had finally come.

Two bullets whisked through the air.

I closed my eyes accepting that it was my judgment day.

CHAPTER TWENTY

Willow

Seeing Grym was like a breath a fresh air.

Seeing Grym was like a saving grace.

Seeing Grym gave me hope for tomorrow.

Grym gave me hope for better days to come. When I untied the ropes around Trinity's wrist, I truly believed that no matter how much fight we had in us, we were destined to die at by Santino's hands. Instead I was offered mercy, in the form of Grym.

My right hand shook as I held Grym's gun in my hand. The concept of time disappeared as I realized that I had taken the life of the man who was readily willing to give mine away. The man that was ready to snatch my husband from me.

No one would take my husband from me, not when I'd just gotten him back.

"Mama, give me the gun."

Holding onto my breath as tightly as I was holding on to my sanity, I tried to make sense of me taking a human life. Was that the feeling Grym had every time he snatched a life away? I didn't have any remorse for my actions. He had set me up to die. He was ready to take the love of my life from me.

The man that risked his life to save mine. I took one to save his.

There was no telling how many he had taken to save mine.

"Willow, please mama. Give me the gun."

My hand trembled as Grym pried the gun from my fingers. As I stared at Wallace's lifeless body surrounded by a pool of blood, I recalled Santino's words. "He was going to shoot you, I had to do it baby."

"I know mama. It's okay."

"He set me up. Wallace set me up. He acted like he was trying to protect me, but he wasn't. He wanted me dead for the insurance money, baby. He was going to kill you, I had to do it."

"Mama,"

Regret filled Grym's eyes as he placed the gun back at his waist. Taking the shirt from his back, he put it on me. He lifted me up into his arms and carried me bridal style out of the warehouse. Green informed to tell him that Honcho, whoever that was, was going to take care of everything at the warehouse and had already taken care of my car. Grym asked G to drive while he sat in the back seat with me cradled in his lap. The ride was silent as I buried my face into Grym's chest. After what seemed like almost a two-hour drive, we were pulling up to my house in Fort Lauderdale. We exited the car, with Grym still carrying me bridal style.

Green had his arms around Trinity, and she was wearing his shirt. He went into his pocket and unlocked the door. "Yeah, I made a key. I wasn't about to keep breaking in like Grym's ass."

I wanted to smile at his joke, but I found it impossible to smile. When we were in, Grym carried me straight into the bathroom. He sat me on me the toilet as he went under sink to get all of the items I used for my bath. When he was done running my bath water, he threw in one of my favorite bath bombs. Grym undressed me and helped me into the tub. I allowed my sore body to be submerged beneath the warm water.

Standing up, Grym lit the candles I had on the sink. As soon he was done, he lathered a washcloth and began to wash my body. His eyes were asking questions his mouth was too afraid to ask. I had answers I was too terrified to voice. We welcomed silence until one of us found the courage to break it.

"Mama, I'm sorry." I shook my head for him to stop but he continued. Grym rested his forehead on mine, "That was it for me. I promise you I'm going legit after this. No more killing. None of that shit. Seeing you shoot Wallace hit differently. I should've protected you. I shouldn't have assumed Santino killed Wallace just because I saw him on the ground. Mama, I am so fucking sorry. I am grateful for you, Willow."

Drops of warm salty water dripped down to my lips. Grym was hurting when he had no reason to. To my knowledge, Grym had never felt any remorse after a kill. To know that he was remorseful for me, opened me up to another level of love. One that very few knew existed, let alone experienced.

"I'm not sorry. You shouldn't be either baby. Wallace set me up. All of it was set up for him to collect on the life insurance policy he took out. He was willing to get me killed. When I saw that gun pointed at you, I did what came naturally. I protected you. I protected my love. Fuck that bitch ass nigga."

He chuckled and pulled away from me, "So you're a savage now, mama?"

"No, you're a savage. I'm riding for love."

"I love you, mama."

"I love you too, baby."

Grym kissed my forehead and continued to bathe me. When he was done, he wrapped me up in a towel to carry me to the bedroom. He laid me across the bed, spread my legs, and licked his pink lips.

"Can I put you sleep mama?"

I nodded as he began to lay a trail of kisses down my stomach to my inner thighs. He pushed my legs further apart, running his tongue up and down my inner thighs. My yoni throbbed as his wet lashes got closer.

"Stop teasing me. Please baby," I pleaded with him.

Grym spread my pussy lips and latched onto my pearl. My eyes rolled to the back as he fingered me. Tears streamed from my eyes as the pleasure his skillful tongue overtook my body. Within a minute I was shuttering as his tongued flicked on my hardened clit.

"I'm about to cum baby."

"Give me my shit mama!" he hummed in my pussy.

On command my body gave into him. As I drifted off into the land of ecstasy, sleep took over. The last thing I remembered was Grym cleaning me up with his tongue, followed by a warm wash cloth.

Grym was many things, and he had done a lot. But at the end of it all, he was mine.

CHAPTER TWENTY-ONE

Grym

After Willow was fast asleep, I shot Green a text. The events of the day wouldn't permit me to sleep. Watching Willow take her step-father's life to save mine wasn't something I took lightly. She kept trying to reassure me she was fine, but no one was fine after taking a life for the first time. Especially not someone like Willow. I had tainted her purity, and that guilt was eating me up alive.

When Green texted me he was outside smoking a blunt, I slipped out the bed, grabbed a bottle of white Henny, and met him outside in the backyard. He sat on one lawn chair while I took the other one.

"Man, nigga let me just say it was my fuck up for not checking to make sure Wallace was dead. The way that fuck nigga was laying, I thought he was."

"On some real shit, I thought he was dead too. Then again, we didn't know that nigga was a threat either."

Willow's recount of Wallace's deal with Santino had me super fucked up in the head. Even though I was suspicious of Santino's movement in regard to Wallace, I didn't think Wallace was going to involve Willow. My only regret was that I wasn't the one that pulled that fucking trigger.

"When Trinity told me, I was stuck for a good five minutes nigga. I couldn't tell if it was the loud or the shit about Wallace."

Chuckling, I took a swig of the Henny. "How she doing?"

"She's handling it a lot better than I am. Seeing her like that fucked with me man. Them niggas had my lady in her fucking bra and panties my nigga. I'm giving up this drug shit. What if the next time it's one of my enemies that come for her? The whole city getting burned down behind that shit."

"I felt that shit G. This shit ain't for us no more. I'm glad she's doing good."

A goofy ass grin spread across his face. "She's doing great my nigga. She had me eat edibles from her ass. My nigga, I don't want to do an edible any other way."

"You nasty as fuck," I said shaking my head.

"Fuck you nigga. My lady's ass tastes lovely. And don't be out here capping like you ain't eating ass."

"Don't worry about what the fuck I do with mine nigga. On some real shit though, retirement is a must. Willow took a life, my nigga."

"No cap, that was some savage shit, Grym. How she doing?"

That was some savage ass shit. Willow saved my life.

Without me having to ask, she proved that she had my back. "She's saying she's good G. You remember the first life you took, were you good after that?"

"It fucked me up for a little while."

"Exactly, she can't just be okay."

"Let me ask you this, though. When you saved my life how did you feel? You got to trust in what she's telling you and watch what she's showing you, Grym."

Thinking back on that night, it was either Green's life or those niggas, and the choice was easy to make. After everything went down, I prayed to God for forgiveness and slept like I did any other night. I did what I had to do. That made me feel better, like Willow would be okay after all. If she wasn't, I was going to be there every step of the way helping her get better. Getting out of the game altogether was at the top of the list.

"I hear what you're saying G. But not only does Trinity have you using big words, she got your ass being wise too," I joked.

"Nigga fuck you."

"Nah, fuck you."

We stayed outside a little longer talking about the plan to leave the life behind us. Honcho had proven himself in a major way by stepping up. He had Willow's car brought to us, and everything was cleaned to G's standard. With him making the decision to retire, he thought it was best to reward Honcho for his loyalty.

Green finished his blunt and we went inside to join Willow and Trinity. The money tempting as fuck, but a real nigga would always choose his wife. Willow was my wife, and I was going to spend the rest my days honoring the vows I made.

Slipping into the bed, I drew her body into mine. I pushed her thick hair out the way and kissed her neck. She moaned while pressing her bare ass on my dick. She knew what she was doing to a nigga, and I was going to give her exactly what her ass was asking for.

"Mmmmm baby," she purred as I entered her from the back. I gripped her neck as she threw her head back. Willow was always on some freaky shit. The way she was throwing it back, we were guaranteed at least two more rounds.

"Shit that pussy super wet baby." Willow's pussy was dripping as I dipped in and out of her tight walls. The tighter I choked her, the wetter her pussy got.

There wasn't a single thing I didn't love about Willow.

She was and forever would be my tranquility in the midst of chaos.

CHAPTER TWENTY-TWO

Willow

Waking up, it felt as though the shackles restraining my heart from putting my all into my marriage, had finally broken. It wasn't until I saw myself without Grym did I fully accept he was the man put on Earth to provide, love, and care for me. Death was truly the only thing that could keep us apart. And it had been moments from ripping us apart.

I saved him.

I saved us.

There was no room for remorse in my heart because I did what Grym would've done for me; what he had done for me. Wallace was my step-father but at the end of it all, he attached a value to my life. A million dollar's worth of value. To me, Grym's life was more valuable than his. I would mourn Wallace only to be able to move on. Without Grym, I'd be losing my better half.

"How are you feeling mama?" I was tucked nicely under Grym as we laid in bed.

"I'm in a good space." Hugging him tighter, I forced my body under his more. I traced the tattoos that decorated his forearms with the tips of my fingers.

"Great dick will do that for you," he quipped.

"Yeah, and fire pussy will have you bringing me breakfast in bed."

"Is that what you want mama?" Grym asked after laying a sweet kiss on my forehead.

"Actually, I want the four of us to go out for once. The best thing for me to do for the day is be normal."

"We can do that mama." Pulling away from me, Grym grabbed his phone from the nightstand to text Green with our lunch plans.

"Me and G need to head back to Miami to finalize a few things. We'll be back in time for lunch."

"That's fine baby." That would give me and Trinity some time to unpack the recent events. Neither Green, nor Grym was willing to let us out of their sights.

"You sure you'll be okay? Maybe it's a better idea if y'all come down with us. What do you think mama?"

"Baby, we'll be fine. Y'all take care of business and come back when y'all are done."

Grym lowered his juicy lips to mine. Our kissed intensified as he dropped his hand to my pussy. I drew back. "Grym, baby, no. I'm sore."

"Let me just give you head mama."

"No baby, that's going lead to us fucking. Hurry back."

"Damn, I didn't ever think I'd see the day you'd deny head."

Giggling I replied, "Ain't nobody denying shit over here, baby. I'm just postponing until later."

I gave him a quick kiss on the lips before getting out of bed. We exchanged our goodbyes and he left out with Green. After I was done with my shower, I got dressed, and joined Trinity in her bedroom. Peeling back the comforter, I got in the bed.

"You're probably tired of being asked, but how are you, Willow?"

Grym asked me that question so many times but I understood why, so Trinity asking me the same, didn't bother me. "Surprisingly, I feel fine. That was some crazy shit and we'll probably have some kind of trauma in the near future. But for right now, I feel fine. You're safe, Grym's safe, and Green's safe."

She nodded. "That was some wild ass shit. You on some gangsta shit now." Trinity's attempt to lighten the mood brought a smile to my face.

"Not at all. Hopefully that's the last time I ever have to hold a gun. Grym mentioned retiring and I want him to but that's something he has to do on his own, for himself."

"Green mentioned that too. Those niggas are known in the streets, giving it up is going to be hard."

Trinity may have thought it was going to be really hard, but I didn't that. Progress allowed your vision to change. It permitted people to grow out of old ways and find value in different things.

"Do you think they'll really do it?" I asked her.

"After we got kidnapped and almost died, hell yeah I believe they will. I'm not saying it'll be easy though. It could've been worse, and with the ties they have its not unlikely something like this could happen again. This time had nothing to do with them but who's to say the next time won't? That's the kind of shit Green was saying to me last night. I just thought I was going to have to box the nigga to knock some sense into him first." Trinity's serious expression brought me to laughter again.

Green and Trinity were a perfect match. They were complex individuals, yet they matched each other's vibes well. Both were crazy as hell, but they were accepting of one another's craziness.

"Well, I'm glad you didn't have to box him. But how are you doing? We went through this together."

"On some real shit Willow, I'm good. I wish I would've been the one to pull the trigger on Wallace's bitch ass but other than that, I'm good."

"I can't believe he played me like that."

"Let me tell you something cousin, a desperate muthafucka will always show you their true colors. That's why I keep my circle small. You, and now Green and Grym. That's all I need until Green traps my ass."

"Trap you?" My eyes narrowed in on Trinity. She was thirty years old and had never mentioned having children. Her choice of words almost had me doubling over in laughter.

"Yes! That's what that nigga said."

"What were his words exactly Trinity?"

She did her best Green impersonation. "Babe don't think you 'bout to have me eating edibles from your ass crack and I'm not going to trap you. Your crazy ass ain't ever leaving me."

No longer able to contain myself, I fell back onto the bed in laughter. I held onto my stomach because everything, from his mannerisms to his voice, she had down to a science.

"Damn, that sounds just like Green."

"Hell yeah it does. But no cap, for the very first time I want the family, husband, and house. And I want all that with Green."

As Trinity continued, I thought more about what the future meant for Grym and I. We were already married and living in two different cities. That had to change and hopefully it would, soon.

CHAPTER TWENTY-THREE

Grym

"We really doing this shit?"

"Hell yeah. Our priorities have changed bro. We want a family. Seeing Willow and Trinity in their underwear, scared as fuck, did something to a nigga. That look Willow had in her eyes is going to haunt me forever," I tossed.

The second we arrived in Miami, I packed a bag to spend a week with Willow until I found a spot in Fort Lauderdale. Truth was, even if she said she was coping fine, there would be days that would be hard to deal with. I wasn't going to subject her to that trauma by having her living in the place where it all happened. That living separately shit was dead though. So I made the decision to move to Fort Lauderdale. I had already gotten my real estate agent looking for a house. In the days leading up to us getting married, Willow described her dream home in detail, and I planned to give her that.

My retiring was different than Green. I did my shit solo. Wasn't nobody eating off me except me. I was my own boss and employee. When I said I was done, I was done. My burner phone was the only line of contact my clients had to me and I had gotten rid of that shit.

After we left my house we went to G's, where he did the same. All the shit he talked about changing for a worthy woman was becoming a reality. My nigga did a whole a one-eighty for Trinity. The shit was crazy to witness, but they were both crazy as hell. Ironically, it made sense that they were able to handle each other.

"You right. Trinity is definitely pregnant."

"Nigga how the hell do you know that she's pregnant. Y'all only been together, what? A month."

"It only takes one nut to have a baby nigga. She's pregnant. Wait and see. I wasn't playing about trapping her ass either. Ya boy done got an engagement ring and all that shit."

"I'm proud of you nigga."

"Appreciate it. I'm proud of you too. Just think about it, if Willow had never blocked your number that night, I wouldn't be having a young jit soon."

"I'm glad I could help," I said while laughing at Green's stupid ass.

There was a knock on the door, Green called for them to come in and Honcho walked in looking exhausted as fuck. I could respect it since he had done a lot in the past twenty-four hours to prove his loyalty. He had always been the type of nigga to keep his head low and work. That nigga wasn't hungry for power. He was hungry to succeed and feed his family.

He was about to reap the rewards of what loyalty meant to me and G.

"You good jit?" Green asked.

"Yeah. I'm super tired but that ain't ever going to stop shit," Honcho said while dapping us up.

Once he was seated, Green continued, "I'm not going to hold you up. Last night put a lot of shit into perspective for me. What I want for my future, the life I'm living can no longer provide it, ya feel me? I'm retiring, all that shit is yours if you want it. Santino is gone but I can get you with a new connect."

Honcho leaned in, more attentive. "You for real? Don't play with a nigga like that."

"Fuck would I play about some shit like that for nigga? Do I look like a nigga that plays game?" Green asked aggressively.

"Nah, it's not that Green. Niggas talk about retiring all the time, I've yet to see one of them go through with that shit."

"Well I ain't any nigga. I'm Green muthafucka," he stated before a loud chuckle erupted from his throat.

"What percentage you want your cut? Twenty?"

That was how I knew Green was handing his legacy to the right nigga. Some niggas were starving for that shit and it made them desperate. They wouldn't even think to give the nigga handing them over everything a percentage.

"That's all you. I'm taking my hands out completely. You a young nigga so I'm going to keep it G with you. When you trying to walk away from something, you have to be completely done with that shit. Don't be one in and one out. It's easy to get pulled back in that way. You got this."

Green took a black duffle bag and threw it at Honcho's feet. "This all the shit you need. Stay hungry and stay loyal nigga."

Standing up, the two exchanged a brotherly hug, and Honcho left. After Green was done smoking his blunt, we headed back to Fort Lauderdale. I shot a quick text to Willow letting her know we were on the way. The drive felt shorter than ever before. Green and I drove separately because we had individual surprises planned after our couples' lunch.

When we made it to Willow and Trinity's house, they were already outside waiting on us. Willow wore a yellow sundress that had me bricked up. She fucked my mind all the way up and I loved it. Getting out the car, I stepped around and opened the passenger side door. As she was getting in, I slapped her ass and held on to her right ass cheek.

"Just know I'm going to fuck you up for that dress."

"I want you to fuck me, baby." She winked at me and sat in her seat. I went around, got in the car, and drove off to a Haitian restaurant Willow was dying to try. Growing up in Little Haiti she was surrounded by Haitian culture and every once in a while, she like indulging. That didn't bother me because Haitian food was good as hell. She told me she could cook a few dishes but until I tried it for myself, I wasn't going to believe it.

The four of us sat at the table waiting for the waitress to return with our food. I had been waiting for this meal the whole day. Willow made a nigga promise not to eat without her, who was I to eat when my woman wanted me to starve because we had a lunch date?

When the food finally came, I didn't even give the waitress time to put it in the table before taking a piece of chicken off my plate.

"Damn nigga you couldn't wait?" Green poked at me.

"Clearly not nigga."

"Ol' hungry ass."

"Bitch ass nigga," I replied.

"Y'all need to stop." Trinity and Willow said together.

The banter between Green and I was nothing new. In fact, it brought us closer. Nothing could fuck up our brotherhood. Sometimes you had to curse you brother out whether it was to get him right or for a laugh.

"Man, I got some shit to do and this nigga messing it up, acting like he ain't ate all day."

Knowing exactly what direction Green was going in, I dropped the piece of chicken on the plate to throw my hand up as a sign of surrendering.

"What's going on?" Trinity asked looking from me to Green.

"Babe, it's only been a month which scares the fuck out of me. If a month is like this, what will a lifetime be like?"

"Daddy…" Trinity started but Green cut her off.

"Babe, you changed a real nigga in so many ways. It may seem crazy but everything about us is crazy. That shit so crazy it makes sense. That's why in front of my brother and your cousin, I'm asking will you do me the honor of becoming my wife?"

Willow jumped out her seat and began clapping drawing everyone's attention to our table. Trinity's hands went up to her mouth as tears rolled down her cheeks. Unable to speak, she nodded as she and Green embraced one another.

As we enjoyed our lunch, Trinity and Willow spent most of the time going over wedding plans. After we finished, Green and Trinity went to celebrate with their edibles. To surprise Willow, I took her back to the park we went to when we agreed to work on us.

The minute we got to the park; I went to the trunk to pull out her favorite blanket. Willow found us a place to sit that was somewhat secluded.

"The park is one of my favorite places."

Gazing into the eyes of the woman that had given me another chance at life, I removed a small black box out of my pocket. Willow had begun wearing her ring again, yet I wanted her to have the wedding she didn't have, the marriage she had envisioned; I wanted her to have all of that and more.

"Willow I want us to purchase the dream home we spoke about. The wedding, the family, the children, you deserve all of that. I love you so much mama. No matter what I do for you, it'll never be enough to repay you for all that you've done for me. You are my heart, my past, my present, and future. Nothing would make me happier than for you to say yes to us renewing our vows. Willow, will you marry me again?"

She wrapped her arms around my neck making it hard for me to breathe. Willow was strong as fuck for her to be so slim. "Mama, you didn't save my life to choke me out, did you?"

Willow released my neck and I saw the widest grin on her face. "Sorry baby. I love you."

"I love you too. What's the answer?"

"Stop playing with me. The answer is yes. The answer will always be yes, baby."

Taking her bottom lip into my mouth. I sucked on it softly. I pulled her on top of me. My dick was at attention and begging me to free him. Scanning to see if anyone was around, I lifted Willow up to release. Like the pro she was, she slid down my dick while tightening her pussy muscles.

"Shit!" Her pussy was so fucking wet, I was ready to drown in that shit.

"How good does it feel baby?"

"Good as fuck mama."

I was killer when it came to Willow. Her spirit was the bullet that pierced me. Her soul was the barrel that sent it flying. And her love.

Her love was the grip that held us together.

The End

OUTRO:

Again, thank you for taking time to read one of my stories. I truly hope you enjoyed Grym and Willow's story. Hopefully, Trinity and Green touched your heart as well. If did, please feel free to leave a review. It would be greatly appreciated it. I chose to end the way I did because this wasn't a book that required an epilogue. And maybe, if the Urban Romance bug bites me again, I may start off where the story ended. Maybe. We'll have to wait and see, won't we?

You can find me on social media such as IG and FB under Ivy Laika to stay connected. Join my Facebook group Laika's Love Lounge.

I would also like to take a moment to thank my sister's in petty Aubree Pynn and Jess Words. Aubree, thank you for creating my vision for the cover of this book. Jess, thank you for working hard on the edits. To my readers, as always, thank you for the continued support. It is not overlooked and it is greatly appreciated.

Until next time.

Signed,

Ivy Laika-Lover of love, Nurturer of souls

OTHER BOOKS BY ME:

Untainted Love

A Love Unrefined (Untainted Love spinoff)

Something Deeper

Feign for Me (For Me Series: Book 1)

Yearn for Me (For Me Series: Book 2)

Feel My Love

Finding Freedom: Wrapped in Love's Armour

Claiming Your Love

However. Forever. : A Christmas Novella

At Love's End: A Novelette

Our Desires

The One I Love

www.ingramcontent.com/pod-product-compliance
Lightning Source LLC
Chambersburg PA
CBHW071420150726
48000CB00001B/422